Family Secrets

I shut the kitchen door behind me and faced my father. "Ever since we were born, you've been stuffing us with the Carlisle heritage, you and Mom. It's what's supposed to make up for being dragged all over the globe with no roots of our own. And all the time it was a big lie. You deliberately deceived us!"

CARLISLE'S HOPE

The First Book in an Exciting New Series

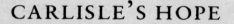

THE CARLISLE CHRONICLES

THE CARLISLE CHRONICLES

CARLISLE'S
HOPE

by Norma Johnston

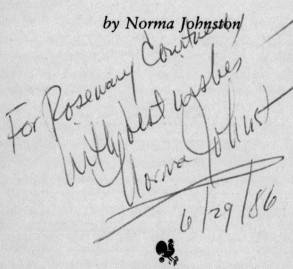

For Rosemary Courtney
With best wishes
Norma Johnst
6/29/86

BANTAM BOOKS
TORONTO · NEW YORK · LONDON · SYDNEY · AUCKLAND

RL 5, IL age 12 and up

CARLISLE'S HOPE
A Bantam Book / May 1986

*Starfire and accompanying logo of a stylized star are registered
trademarks of Bantam Books, Inc. Registered in U.S. Patent and
Trademark Office and elsewhere.*

ISBN 0-553-25467-7

Published simultaneously in the United States and Canada

---

*Bantam Books are published by Bantam Books, Inc. Its trade-
mark consisting of the words "Bantam Books" and the por-
trayal of a rooster, is Registered in U.S. Patent and Trademark
Office and in other countries. Marca Registrada. Bantam
Books, Inc., 666 Fifth Avenue, New York, New York 10103.*

PRINTED IN THE UNITED STATES OF AMERICA

O   0 9 8 7 6 5 4 3 2 1

*In memory
of the grandmother
I never knew—
Catherine A. I. Dryden Chambers Johnston*

ONE

THE SECOND Wednesday in September was a typical Carlisle morning. At thirteen minutes after seven my sister Tracy, who's a high school senior, was standing by the kitchen sink chugalugging coffee; blow-drying her hair (a kitchen activity that drives Dad wild); and talking on the phone to her boyfriend, Bruce Barillo. Scott, a year younger, was wandering around fully dressed, a sandwich in one hand and an electronics magazine in the other, fully engrossed in both. Scott's days never have enough hours in them, and he considers sandwiches to be great time savers.

Today's sandwich was a creative experiment

in leftover pâté, pickles, and smelly cheese, and Susan was making some awful faces over it. Sue—excuse me, Suzi—is thirteen going on thirty—"if she lives that long," as Dad has observed on more than one occasion. Suzi is in eighth grade, majoring in men and possibly a few other things we're afraid to think about.

I was sitting at the kitchen table eating yogurt and worrying about my latest English essay. "Write about a shared family experience that's meant a lot to you," Mr. Eagleton had commanded. Since several of those are sworn family secrets, I'd decided to write about my first significant encounter with Aunt Faith, and now I wasn't sure whether I'd done it justice or told too much.

I should add that I'm Jess (short for Jessamyn, after a writer Mom admires), I'm fifteen, and I'm at the beginning of my sophomore year at Evesham Hall.

The youngest member of our family, Samuel J. Featherstone III, a two-year-old apricot standard poodle who thinks he's a butterfly, was trying to climb into our laps and was stealing toast when he hoped no one was looking. Fortunately Dad and Mother weren't. They were too busy wondering whether there was something wrong with them because they were still married.

"To each other!" Mother tried to sound appalled. "For twenty years! Do you realize we're the only couple we know who hasn't split up *once*? I wonder if it's Freudian."

"Maybe it's because we're crazy," Dad said, leering. He pinched her rump. Mother slapped his hand away.

"If you mean crazy about each other, that's old-fashioned!" Mother considered. "If you mean crazy as in crazy, you have a point."

None of us batted an eye at this conversation. It was the result of the party they'd been to last night. Also at the party had been their friend Paulina Payne, a fifty-year-old flake who's on her third divorce, and Bruce Barillo's mother, Caroline. Caroline's a widow, and a doll, but she's dating an impossibly possessive divorced Greek named Nick Buyukas. As soon as Tracy put down the phone Paulina would probably be on it to pour out to Mom whatever traumas she forgot to confide last night. As I said, it was a typical day around the Carlisle house.

I should say, around the *Flounder* House. As Dad has remarked to me at times, a bit too pointedly, it's a very appropriate place for some of us— meaning me—to live in. Our house is one room wide and four stories high and was built in Old Town, the historic district of Alexandria, Virginia, in the 1780s. It has no windows down one long side, which is why it's called a flounder house. (The flounder's a fish that has both eyes on one side.) In

3

the days flounder houses were built, taxes were based on the amount of costly glass involved, and prudent householders were willing to have one-sided views rather than pay the price of an all-round perspective. That was what Dad was referring to when he said the house was appropriate for me. I don't care; this house makes me feel secure. There are times I think of it as a beautiful shell that I can crawl into and be safe.

Like Aunt Faith's house, Carlisle's Hope, out near New Hope, Pennsylvania, this one has *roots*, and even if it doesn't have Carlisle roots like her house has, I love the feeling of tapping into them. Maybe that matters so much because I'm a Foreign Service kid and till five years ago I lived all over the Middle East. Tracy and Scott and Suzi were born overseas, too, but they *love* being footloose. Maybe I'm just the family-heritage nut of my generation the way Aunt Faith is of hers. . . . Maybe Dad's right, and sometimes I feel like a flounder.

Tracy put down the phone. "Guess what? Caroline's thinking of going to Florida with you-know-who next weekend. And you-know-who's at her again to sell her house. He says there's no point in hanging on to it for the boys. He says she should move into a condo and think of herself. Meaning him. Bruce is having fits."

Mother groaned. "Doug, isn't there *somebody* less neurotic we can introduce Caroline to?"

Dad, turning to the international news in *The*

Washington Post, got a gleam in his eye. "Well, if Caroline were in Beirut, or if Ali were in town—"

"There's nothing romantic about Beirut these days, and our pal Ali's the last thing Caroline needs as an antidote to Nick Buyukas." Mother's own eyes were glinting. "Now, on the other hand, Paulina—"

The telephone rang. Suzi and Featherstone dived for it; Suzi won. "Yeeessss?" she breathed into it throatily. And then, in her normal voice: "Jess, it's Steff."

Stephanie Payne, Paulina's daughter, is one of my two best friends, and her life is a perpetual trauma. A call from her right before we were due to meet at school could mean trouble. The more matter-of-fact I was, the better, I decided. "Hi," I said brightly. "Did you get your essay for English done?"

"What? Oh—yes." Stephanie had that little catch in her voice that I recognized with a sinking heart. "I wrote about Christmas at Grandmother Winkler's when I was six. At least I think it was Grandmother Winkler's. The one who lived up in Boston and took us to hear the handbell choir." As I said, the Paynes have been through a lot of divorces and remarriages. "What did you write about?" she asked me.

"Aunt Faith's farm, and what it felt like the first time I saw it, that night we came home from Beirut when I was ten." I heard a choking sound on the other end of the line. "Steff, what's wrong?" I asked quickly.

"I thought I'd better warn your mother. Mom slammed out of here two minutes ago, and I think she's on her way over there. She was popping Valiums at breakfast. Your mother'd better get ready." Stephanie hung up abruptly.

Around me in the kitchen the pleasurable hum of sound had come to an abrupt halt. Even Featherstone was silent.

"Paulina?" Scott asked, not without sympathy. I nodded.

"Stephanie thinks she's on her way here. If she can drive straight."

Mother and Dad exchanged worried glances. "I don't dare stay. I have an early meeting," Dad said, fishing for his car keys. "Any of you guys want a ride?"

"Bruce is driving me," Tracy said immediately. Bruce was a year older than Tracy, a college freshman. He had his own car and his own apartment.

Scott was meeting friends at the bus stop, but Suzi and I accepted.

"As soon as I'm dressed!" Suzi shouted, diving for the door. I was already in my Evesham Hall uniform, which fortunately did not look *too* much like a uniform. Actually the camel-colored skirt and dark brown jacket could almost pass for normal clothes, and it's my hard luck that I inherited Dad's black hair and olive skin instead of Mother's ash-blond-streaked-with-honey hair, which would have gone so much better with the brown and camel. Tracy's hair is a perfect match for the brown jacket, and as for Suzi, who's black-and-olive too, there hasn't been an outfit made yet that could look bad on her.

"I still don't see why we couldn't have gone to public school," I said absently, and Dad answered, equally force-of-habit, "You know why. Because you came from private schools overseas and the curriculums are similar, and we didn't know how soon you might be overseas again. Besides, practically everybody around here goes to private schools."

Dad's something called a Senior Service Officer with the U.S. Information Agency, which explains why we lived in the Middle East till Dad got yanked home at the time of the Iranian hostage crisis.

The telephone rang again. "I'll get it," I said, snatching it up quickly. I was so prepared to hear Stephanie's voice that for a minute the voice I did hear didn't register. It was half deep, yet half uncertain, like a child's. What it was saying was "Aunt Jenetta?"

"No, it's Jess." My head cleared. "John Henry, is that *you*?"

I sensed, rather than saw, my parents straighten. Tracy and Scott moved closer to the phone.

"Uh-huh." My ten-year-old cousin gulped, then his voice came again in those deep tones that amused us because they were so like his father's. Only they weren't funny now. "Can Uncle Doug call my dad? Mom—*Mom*—"

"What's the matter with Aunt Faith?"

Out of the corner of my eye I saw my parents streaking for the family-room extension. I heard Tracy gasp. Scott sat on the table, the half-eaten sandwich forgotten in his hand.

I forced my voice to calm down. "John Henry, hang on. Dad'll be on the line in a second."

"I am on," Dad said matter-of-factly. "John Henry, tell me what has happened."

What had happened didn't seem real, not even when I heard my own voice, unnaturally high, speaking the words aloud to Scott and Tracy.

"Aunt Faith . . . was in an automobile accident last night. They don't know if she'll live."

TWO

AUNT FAITH was in the intensive-care unit of a hospital near New Hope and needed immediate radical surgery. But the doctors needed permission from her next of kin, and Uncle Henry—Colonel Henry Squier, USAF (ret.)—was somewhere out of the country on a fact-finding mission for the Pentagon.

I heard all this as though from far away: John Henry, very stiff-upper-lip, trying to live up to being "the colonel's kid"; Mother on another extension (she must have rushed upstairs); and Dad saying, "Give us the name of the hospital again, son. Do you have the phone number? Good. I'll talk to the doctors, then I'll call your dad. He can be home by midnight. I'll be there myself on the next plane. I'm your mom's brother; I can give permission. Have you got anybody standing by you?"

John Henry, voice cracking, said, "Yes, a neighbor." I just stood there listening, saying nothing. Tracy came over and rubbed my shoulders. Suzi, now dressed, charged in, slamming on the brakes when she saw us. I heard Scott telling her in a low voice what had happened. The phone line went dead. Tracy took the receiver from me and set it in its cradle.

"Jessamyn! Susan! I'm leaving now. If you're coming, come!" Dad roared.

We came.

Nobody said much. Suzi looked scared; Dad deeply worried. We drove carefully around the hairpin curves through the Virginia countryside, lovely with end of summer, and where horses were galloping in paddocks I saw a vision of Aunt Faith, slim and young in jeans with her head back laughing, trying to get a saddle on her gelding. Where the asters and the Virginia bluebells were blooming, I saw Aunt Faith gathering herbs and wild flowers in her farmhouse garden. My eyes were stinging, and I was gripping my notebook tightly. Tentatively Suzi's hand touched mine.

"Want me to tell the kids for you?" she asked. Everyone knew that while we all loved Aunt Faith, it was me for whom she was soul mate, role model, fairy godmother. I shook my head.

"Let's not say anything unless we have to." The last thing I wanted was to talk about Aunt Faith, unless she came through the operation all right. *Until* she came through the operation all right. I flinched from the alternative.

We drove through Evesham Hall's exceedingly imposing gates. We came to a stop before Evesham Hall's stupendous Tudor main building. "I'll call your mother as soon as I've seen Faith's doctors," Dad said. He was impatient to get to his office, call off his meeting, start the wheels turning for his sister. But I would have to go through the motions of classes, feeling angrily helpless. Suzi gave me an uncharacteristic hug and vanished toward the middle school building. I could hear two of the guys from Evesham's brother school, Cheltenham, calling to her as I turned inside.

Evesham is technically all female and Cheltenham all male, which is a farce. They're on the same grounds, they have the same board of directors, and we share classes and the cafeteria. The technical separation has something to do with sentimental old grads and a lot more to do with a complicated legal situation with endowments. None of that stops the student bodies from mingling in the classrooms and, even more successfully, outside. So when Alaiyo Webster, my other best friend, came hurrying across Evesham's Great Hall toward me, she was predictably not alone. Karim Asagai towered over her.

Asagai's a senior, a diplomat's son, and a black Adonis, which goes a long way in explaining why Alaiyo has been calling herself Alaiyo these days instead of Lee Anne, her baptismal name. Her parents, who are justly proud of a family heritage as distinguished black American intellectuals, are baffled. I wondered whether Alaiyo had told her mother yet that she planned on wearing African robes to the school dance that weekend. She'd look gorgeous in them.

"Jess, there's a dance-committee meeting after school today. Can you stay?" Alaiyo called. And at that moment Stephanie arrived, looking like death warmed over, and I was spared explaining why I wouldn't want to hang around after school. Alaiyo and I exchanged glances and closed in on Steff, and Asagai excused himself with a courteous smile. Stephanie looked at me, stony-faced.

"Did my mother show up at your place?"

"Not yet. Don't worry. If she's not there within the hour, my mom will send out the Marines."

"If she's not already smashed up somewhere," Stephanie said sharply.

"Okay, girl, what happened?" Alaiyo asked.

"She's stoned," Stephanie replied uncompromisingly. We didn't need her to explain that *she* meant Paulina. "Stoned, soused, sozzled, whatever you want to call it. She didn't get home till four A.M., and I was up the whole time waiting for her. You don't know what it's like to be waiting for a call about whether somebody's alive or dead."

Oh, don't I? I thought bitterly, and then felt ashamed. "Don't go expecting the worst." I was reassuring myself as well as her. "Paulina's not really in that bad shape, is she?"

"I wish I knew. *She* sure thinks she isn't. At least where pill popping and swilling are concerned." The crude words were a harsh contrast to Stephanie's fragile blondness, but Stephanie's been dealing with a lot of reality since her latest stepfather walked out.

"Steff," Alaiyo said gently, "we've told you a hundred times. You can't save people from themselves. You have to wait till they hit rock bottom and wake up on their own."

"It's easy for you to talk!" Stephanie flashed. "*Your* family's respectable. You don't have any drunks or pill poppers or divorces. Neither do the Carlisles."

"Unless you count Suzi," I said apprehensively. "I wouldn't bank on anything where Suzi's concerned."

"She's got too much sense of self-preservation," Stephanie said flatly. "And she's a Carlisle. What's that old Carlisle family motto you're always quoting? See? You even have a motto, and a war cry, and a survive-and-conquer record going back to the Scottish clans. So do the Websters—"

"But not Scottish," Alaiyo interrupted firmly.

"Okay, okay, Ashanti or Bantu or whatever. You know what I mean," Stephanie said doggedly, her violet eyes glistening. "A tradition, a family backbone to lean on and live up to. I don't even have a last name!" Paulina had made Stephanie change that regularly with each new marriage. "I wonder what we're going back to this time," Stephanie added grimly. "Mother's maiden name? She can't go back to being a fifty-year-old virgin, not with me around!" She drew in a deep ragged breath. "Maybe we'd both be happier if she did wind up in a ditch!"

"Oh, *shut up!*" I burst out violently.

Both girls stared at me, and I hugged myself hard to keep from shaking. Now it was too late for secrecy. "Aunt Faith got smashed up in a car accident last night," I said thickly. "Bad. And if either of you says one more word to me, I—I don't know what I'll do."

And then in the shocked silence I looked ahead and saw Greg Barillo, Bruce's younger brother, ambling through the hall's main door, relaxed and at home with himself and the world. And I walked through the little corridor that opened up between us and said to him, "What's this I hear about you guys moving?"

It was so weird. I didn't plan it; I couldn't

have imagined myself doing it, walking up to a boy I barely knew and talking to him like that. Besides, I was pretty sure that the subject was a sore one. It was the kind of outgoing thing Aunt Faith would have done. But I saw myself doing it, saw the girls watching me, too stunned to follow.

Greg didn't mind though. He looked at me and grinned, his blue eyes humorous below his thatch of brown hair. "Don't count on it. Mom gets carried away sometimes, but not *that* far away. Why worry about things that may never happen?" Then he took my books and walked me to our English lit class, which he's taking for the fun of it even though he's a junior. Greg Barillo, who has the reputation for being either the shyest, the most aloof, or the least girl-crazy—take your pick—boy at Cheltenham.

His calmness was a rock to lean on, and I leaned on it most of the day. Maybe he knew I needed it. Maybe he'd been waiting for me to make the first move (an interesting idea I'd think about later, when I felt better). Whatever, he walked me to my second-period class, and he showed up at lunch to suggest eating under the willow tree in the courtyard. Steff and Alaiyo had the tact not to join us.

I didn't call Mom for news as I had planned to. I avoided Suzi. I blotted out images of Aunt Faith and cut my English comp class at which I might have had to read that composition about her. Instead, I sat on a sun-dappled rock with Greg (who wasn't cutting; he had Free Study) and discussed *Great Expectations* (he loved it; I didn't) and the parts of Dickens's London I could remember from when I'd been there with my parents.

When it was time for us to go to our last classes of the day, Greg cleared his throat. "That *Great Expectations* test tomorrow. Maybe we could study for it tonight together."

"Maybe we could," I said demurely, but my heart was singing. I was absolutely, totally aware just then of nothing but Greg's crooked smile and the way he managed to look comfortably rumpled in Cheltenham's required jacket and tie.

That sense of security enveloped me like a cocoon as I floated into poli sci, and it enveloped me on the school bus as I rode home. Suzi sat in the back with her friends and did not intrude; Stephanie and Alaiyo went home by different bus routes.

I got off at the usual corner of King Street and headed home—along the familiar, centuries-old, cobbled streets; beneath the gas lampposts and the summer-green trees; past the boutiques and the prim Federal town houses and the tourists.

I went up the two steps to our bright blue front door, my mouth open to tell Mom the interesting news that Greg Barillo had invited himself over that night.

And my mother met me in the front hall to tell me that Aunt Faith had died.

THREE

I DIDN'T have my study date with Greg that night.

It was Scott who phoned him. Scott, who was Greg's best friend. That was after Suzi had come meandering into the house after me, and stopped dead when she saw the expression on my mother's face.

"Why?" I demanded tightly.

Mother shook her head. "Wait till the others get here. I don't think I can go through it more than once." She moved into the kitchen and we followed her. I remember wishing it were cold enough for a fire in the fireplace. Mother put the copper kettle on for tea—a Carlisle crisis custom, generations old. By the time it was whistling, Scott had arrived with Bruce and Tracy.

"Faith never regained consciousness," Mother said. "Something about a blood clot in her brain."

"I thought they were going to operate!" I burst out.

"They did. Your father gave permission by way of the computer in his office, and she was on the operating table when he got out there. He telephoned when the operation was completed, then he telephoned again an hour ago to say she'd died."

Something cold and wet touched my cheek. Featherstone, trying to lick comfort into me. I pushed him away. "This stupid government work! If Uncle Henry hadn't been over in Japan, he could have given permission for the operation right away! They wouldn't have had to call all over the world trying to locate a relative. Just like all the times Dad—"

"*Jessamyn!*" I had rarely heard Mother's voice like that. She paused, then went on evenly. "The surgeon said that by the time Aunt Faith reached the hospital there had already been massive brain damage. All they could have saved was her life, but she would probably have been a vegetable. Would you really have wished that on Faith?"

I couldn't answer. It wasn't fair. Nothing was fair.

"Up the Carlisles," Suzi quoted deliberately, exactly as Dad would have done. It was the family way of running up the flag. Carlisles did what had to be done; Carlisles didn't break; Carlisles survived.

"So what now?" Scott asked practically. Mother looked grateful.

"There's a plane to Philadelphia around six. Dad will meet us at the airport and drive us to Carlisle's Hope. Your uncle Henry can't get here till tomorrow morning, so he wants Dad to . . . go ahead and make arrangements. And he wants John Henry to have family with him."

"Poor kid," Scott said. "What'll happen to him now?"

"We'll bring him back with us probably. Unless Henry's thinking of taking him to Japan. His work there won't be done till Christmas."

I had a sudden vivid picture of Aunt Faith's farm, closed and empty, at that most special time of year. No more Aunt Faith winding the stairrails with garlands of small red apples and pine and holly. No more watching Aunt Faith paint in her barn studio. No more laughing with Aunt Faith, or confiding in Aunt Faith, or sharing secrets with Aunt Faith.

Suzi stood up. "I'll go pack. I'll pack for you guys too, if you want."

"I can do my own," I said curtly.

"Featherstone," Mother said blankly. We

looked at him trying to be ingratiating, lying on his back with all four feet in the air. "The kennel won't take him on this short notice."

"If you want, I'll move in and look out for him while you're gone," Bruce offered.

"Please. And tell your mother what happened." Mother stood still, looking around with an indecisiveness that was somehow shocking. "Paulina—I told Paulina to come over here for dinner. And I have an article due at the *Times* on Monday."

"I'll call them," Tracy said firmly. "I'll call everybody who's listed on the calendar, and I'll tell them to call anybody else who ought to know we're going away. Now, go get ready." Mother was still in the worn-out jeans and old shirt that were her uniform while writing. She nodded vaguely and went upstairs.

I just stood. I didn't call Greg; I didn't call Alaiyo. I moved like an automaton when somebody prodded me, and changed out of my uniform under Tracy's guidance. Eventually Bruce drove us all to National Airport in our shabby station wagon. We must have eaten dinner on the plane. I don't remember. I don't remember anything until we were in a rented car, with Dad at the wheel, driving up through the dark to the front door of Carlisle's Hope, and Aunt Faith wasn't there.

The old house screamed her absence. No lights were on, pouring out a welcome. No candles were lit in the tall brass sticks on the hall table. No tantalizing whiffs of cinnamon were drifting from the kitchen. I always associated Aunt Faith with the scent of cinnamon and cloves. The low-ceilinged rooms were stiff and formal. Then I saw Aunt Faith's sketch pad, laid down carelessly with her reading glasses on the study hassock. She'd been making a sketch for a children's book illustration, a sketch that looked uncannily like me when I was small, and for a minute I could not breathe.

"John Henry's sleeping next door with a friend," Dad said. "I *hope* he's sleeping. He was awakened at two A.M. last night by police coming to report the accident." So John Henry had won the battle he'd been having when we were here last summer to convince his parents that ten years old was old enough to be home alone in the evening without a sitter, I realized.

I don't remember much else about that evening except crawling into one of the big canopied beds with Suzi, and Suzi asking awkwardly, "Want to talk?"

"No." I wished I hadn't been so blunt, but Suzi understood.

In the morning there was chaos—telephoning and trips to the funeral home and visitors coming in. Aunt Faith had so many friends. There were flowers and telegrams and phone calls. The newspapers had picked up the accident from the police blotter.

"We kind of forget Faith Carlisle's a pretty big name as an illustrator," Scott said dazedly, after keeping a TV crew from bothering our uncle and John Henry. "Not to mention being Colonel Squier's wife, of course."

"Not to mention being young and beautiful and talented and dead," I said viciously, staring at the self-portrait in the hall that the TV crew had received permission to photograph.

Scott looked at me. "Cool it," he said deliberately.

"What do you mean?"

"You know what I mean. We're all crazy about Aunt Faith, but she's not our mother. She's John Henry's mother and Uncle Henry's wife. And it might make things easier for them if you weren't taking everything so personally."

I was outraged. "Scott Thomas Carlisle! I haven't even cried!"

"Maybe it would do you more good if you did. What good does it do to get mad at Aunt Faith for dying?"

I didn't hit him. I turned on my heel, and went out to the meadow, and wrestled with my soul. And I was not proud of what I saw.

Uncle Henry came home, very military even in his civilian suit. He looked gray; he looked old. I had never been so conscious of the fact that he was almost twenty years older than Aunt Faith. Even a year or so older than my dad.

The old family stories came back to me: how my grandfather Charles Edward Carlisle had died of a heart attack at fifty-three (just two years older than Dad was now!), leaving Dad at eighteen to look after his mother and Aunt Faith, who was only two. Dad's sister, my aunt Meg, was already married and had moved to California. Gadge, my grandmother Carlisle, had gone back to a business career until she retired to Florida.

I wondered whether Gadge and Aunt Meg were coming for the funeral.

It was Dad who had really been a father to Aunt Faith. When he'd been stationed overseas and she'd gotten in trouble with those radical student groups, he'd practically torn his hair out. When she'd started developing a market for her artwork, he'd been so proud. When she'd married Uncle Henry, after meeting him at our house in Cairo, he'd been relieved. Uncle Henry adored Aunt Faith. Everybody adored Aunt Faith. That was why Carlisle's Hope was like a three-ring circus now.

Sometime that afternoon, Uncle Henry disappeared. He came back carrying an armful of heavy cloth. "Faith would have wanted this flying," he said, and he and John Henry ran it up the flagpole. The Carlisle clan banner.

Up the Carlisles, I thought.

Gadge flew in from Florida. Aunt Meg couldn't come, but her daughter and son-in-law—

my cousins Carol and Peter from New Jersey—did. We got through the interminable condolences, the visiting hours, the funeral. There wasn't a grave- side service. Aunt Faith had been cremated, as she'd wanted. I almost wished there *had* been a burial. Seeing a casket lowered into the ground would have put a finish to the nightmare. This way I kept expecting to see Aunt Faith walk through some door.

I didn't crack. I never cracked. Not once.

Now it was Sunday. The family was dispers- ing. Dad had to get back to D.C. for meetings, and Mother had to finish that free-lance assignment for the *Times*. John Henry was coming with us, for how long we did not yet know, and Scott was help- ing him to pack. I could hear their voices, sounding matter-of-fact in the next room, as I packed my bag. Outside the window Aunt Faith's gelding, Sil- ver, was galloping round the paddock. One of the neighbors was going to take care of him and the cats. Downstairs Dad's voice, and Mother's, and Uncle Henry's drifted up through the heating vent in the floor. They were discussing Carlisle's Hope.

"It was Faith's house," Uncle Henry said. "I know it belonged to all three of you technically, but it was Faith's place." There were murmurs of assent. "I don't know when or whether I'll be able to tolerate it again," Uncle Henry said heavily.

"You can always live here," Dad said. "I talked to Meg about it, and she agrees. Whenever you like, as long as you like. And John Henry, of course. We've always felt we'd keep the place for the next generation."

"I've always thought it's Jess who will end up here," Uncle Henry said unexpectedly. "You can see what the place means to her. I suppose it's because she has a need for roots, just as Faith did. Which reminds me." I heard a chair creak, and Uncle Henry's footsteps leaving; climbing one flight of stairs and another, up to the attic.

I threw myself down on my great-grand-mother Faith Carlisle's hand-stitched Star of Bethlehem quilt and I bawled.

I was still bawling when a knock sounded on the door. I dried my eyes hastily.

Uncle Henry came in and tactfully ignored my tears. "I thought you might like to have this. Faith found it in the attic and meant to give it to you." He held out a small mahogany box inlaid with fruitwood. "There are some family papers in it. Nothing valuable, and nothing more than a hundred years old, but she thought you'd like them. She only gave them a once-over lightly."

I cleared my throat. "Uncle Henry, do you think I could have this quilt?"

"I don't see why not. Faith was given it because she was named for her grandmother, and Faith's your middle name." He gave me one of his rare, shy smiles, handed me the wooden box, and departed.

I didn't look in the box. I stuffed it away in my suitcase, folded the quilt up carefully, and got ready to go home.

It was late Sunday evening when we reached the Flounder House. *Now* there were candles, *now* there were fires burning. Bruce must have kindled one in every fireplace in the house. His mother was there, too, and Greg, and—more to the point—an enormous pan of lasagna. We all discovered we were ravenous.

It wasn't till I was up on the third floor, in my own room, that I remembered Uncle Henry's box again. By then it was very late, and the whole house was supposedly asleep. I could hear Featherstone snoring on Suzi's bed next door. The fire in my bedroom fireplace had died down to embers, but the candles still burned bravely on the dark red mantel. The Star of Bethlehem quilt flaunted its pinks and oranges and golds across my bed.

Up the Carlisles, I thought.

I got the box from my suitcase and crawled with it back in bed. A faint whiff of clove and cinnamon wafted out as I raised the lid.

There were papers, and brittle envelopes, and photographs. One was of a sweet-faced young girl with dark wavy hair and her head tilted to one side—Great-grandmother Faith Carlisle; I recognized her from one of Aunt Faith's paintings. It had been done from a photograph, because she had died before Gadge and Grandpa Carlisle ever met.

Dad's father, like Dad himself, had been on his own while young.

Like John Henry was now. *Up the Carlisles.* The Carlisles could survive.

I opened the first letter, which was addressed to my grandfather Carlisle, and glanced at it vaguely.

And then I looked again.

OFFICE OF
PROTHONOTARY
COURT OF COMMON PLEAS
ALLEGHENY COUNTY
PITTSBURGH, PA.

Oct. 15, 1942

C. E. Carlisle
c/o New York Telephone Company
Room 1900
101 Willoughby Street
Brooklyn, New York

Dear Sir:

In reply to yours of 13th inst.

There is no record in our files of any adoption of Charles Edward Carlisle by Douglas Scott Carlisle during the period you indicated, 1906–1908.

The marriage records do record a marriage between Faith Dryden and Douglas Scott Carlisle at Trinity Evangelical and Reformed

Church, Wilkinsburg, Allegheny County, Pennsylvania, on April 25, 1906.

My grandfather Charles Edward Carlisle had been born on December 2, 1897. That was nine years *before* Faith Dryden married Douglas Scott Carlisle.

My grandfather was somebody else's son. He wasn't a Carlisle. He had never been a Carlisle. *We* weren't Carlisles.

Up the Carlisles . . . the family's backbone, the family's roots, the family's flag of pride. Everything my father, everything *Aunt Faith*, had taught me to hold on to and believe in, weren't really mine at all.

FOUR

I couldn't grasp the implications of what I had just seen. I didn't want to grasp them. My mind slammed the door on them as sharply, as involuntarily, as my fingers slammed shut the lid of the inlaid box.

Suddenly, despite all that lasagna, I was hungry. Suddenly nothing mattered as much as getting downstairs and raiding that comforting, familiar refrigerator in our comforting, familiar kitchen. I slid out from under the Star of Bethlehem quilt, into a robe and slippers, and out into the shadowy hall. The robe was quilted and the house was warm, but I was shivering.

I tiptoed down the two flights of stairs, avoiding the steps that creaked, and I was into the lighted kitchen before I realized that it was not empty. Side by side like two solemn old men, John Henry Squier and Samuel J. Featherstone III sat waiting for a saucepan of milk to come to a boil.

I took one look at my cousin's face and got myself under stern control.

"Hi," I said matter-of-factly. "You guys hungry too? There's some of Caroline's chocolate cake in the pantry."

"I woke up," John Henry said gruffly. "Mom always says hot milk's the best thing for getting back to sleep." He was still using the present tense, I noticed. He noticed too and gulped. Just then the milk started to foam, and John Henry jumped to rescue it, his back to me. "I guess Featherstone can't sleep either. He came too. . . . I'm not hungry, thanks."

"Well, I'm sure *Featherstone* is. And Mom's trying to teach him he can eat only when we do, so we'd better force ourselves."

I got out Caroline's cake, and cut three pieces, and took down Great-grandmother Faith Carlisle's Limoges dessert plates—for us, not Featherstone. Mother always used them when she thought our souls needed nurturing.

John Henry divided the hot milk carefully between a mug for himself and Featherstone's bowl. Featherstone was enthusiastic, because he adores milk. He's not supposed to have it since it doesn't always agree with him, but I didn't say a word. And I didn't say a word when John Henry slipped three-quarters of his piece of cake under the table after Featherstone had polished off his own piece in two gulps.

Featherstone laid his head in my lap and I scratched his ears. John Henry scratched his back just above his pompon tail, and Featherstone groaned with ecstasy. It was nice that somebody was happy, I thought.

I glanced at John Henry. "Better get back to bed before the hot milk wears off. You'll have to be up early to register for school tomorrow." Not tomorrow, I realized. Today. It was two A.M.

"I don't know if it makes sense to start school here," John Henry said carefully. "My dad'll probably come for me real soon."

His dad was already on the other side of the world and wasn't going to be able to get back to Pennsylvania for at least two months. He wasn't apt to *stay* in Pennsylvania anyway—not for a long while, if ever. I knew those things, if John Henry didn't.

I knew too much.

I rose abruptly. "Come on," I said. I put the saucepan in the sink to soak, turned out the light, and pushed Featherstone and John Henry ahead of me up the stairs. John Henry looked awfully little, starting alone up the last flight. "You can crawl in with Scott—if you're cold up there, I mean," I added hastily. "Scott won't mind." We had settled John Henry into the back room of Scott's attic kingdom.

John Henry nodded solemnly and plodded on up. Featherstone looked after him, then at me, and marched firmly into my bedroom and jumped up on the bed. I took the hint and followed. We snuggled down with Great-grandmother Carlisle's quilt.

Only she wasn't really my great-grandmother, was she? None of us were blood kin of the Carlisles at all.

To blot out thought I concentrated on Featherstone's heavy breathing, and the next thing I knew, the sun was streaming into my room, along with the smell of my father's hair-stand-on-end coffee.

It was again one of those typical Carlisle mornings. Dad stood clutching a coffee cup in one hand and the telephone in the other. Mother ate while making notes prior to calling *The Washington Post*. Scott was fixing a sandwich, and Featherstone was stealing food. Anybody who didn't know us well would have thought it was just another day. And I was back to feeling like a flounder. Or maybe an ostrich trying to hide its head in the sand.

Meanwhile Featherstone was *really* trying to hide his head—under the tablecloth, so Mother wouldn't see the blueberry muffin he'd snitched off John Henry's plate. But his apricot rump stuck up in the air, his tail wagging ecstatically. Mother gave the tail an absent tweak.

"That dog acts starved," she said. "I can't believe Bruce didn't come by and feed him. We *did* remember to give him his dinner last night, didn't we?"

John Henry's eyes and mine met guiltily, and John Henry gave me a halfway grin. For an instant Aunt Faith's mischief was in his eyes.

"All right! I'll be there as soon as I can make it!" Dad dropped the receiver into its cradle and turned to Mother. "I'll take the subway; it's faster than driving into D.C. during rush hour. Can you run me to the station in ten minutes?"

Mother was already dialing the phone herself. "I need time to dress. I have to look respectable to register John Henry at Cheltenham."

"The kid's big enough to register himself, Ma. I'll be there to help him." Scott's eyes met Mother's, and he gave John Henry a gentle cuff. "Come on. I'll show you what to wear your first day." John Henry, grateful at being rescued from an unwanted breakfast, followed Scott.

Mother sighed. "That child's wound tighter than a watch spring, and I don't know what to do."

"I'll try to talk to him tonight," Dad said. "If he'll talk. He's like his father, and you know what a Great Stone Face Henry is. Not to mention Faith. For all her openness she could be a regular sphinx when she didn't want to share."

"Carlisle stubbornness," Mother murmured.

It isn't Carlisle, something in me almost shouted. Wherever the family pigheadedness comes from, it isn't from the Carlisles! How could my parents go on talking that way? Unless they didn't know—

And how could they talk about *Aunt Faith* that way?

In books grief's supposed to kill your appetite, so you get all pale and interesting-looking. Grief and unhappiness always affected Stephanie that way. But I was absolutely ravenous, stuffing my face with scrambled eggs and blueberry muffins. And I was creating an invisible little box for myself, pulling the walls in after me. Fortunately nobody noticed.

Mother put on her jeans and drove Dad to the subway station. Tracy battled Suzi for the phone and called Bruce, as though she hadn't kissed him good-night just a few hours ago. Scott shepherded John Henry downstairs in something that was as close to the Cheltenham uniform as he could manage on short notice. And Tracy and Suzi and I fought for mirror space and fixed our hair and dressed. Then we walked down to the bus station and rode to school.

Stephanie and Alaiyo were waiting for me.

"Steff told me about your aunt. I'm sorry," Alaiyo said, and began at once to talk about a school assignment.

So the grapevine—starting with the call to tell Paulina not to come for dinner that night—had done its work. I wouldn't have to talk about Aunt Faith. I wouldn't be tempted to mention the secret of the inlaid box. On any other day Steff and Alaiyo would have guessed from my silence that something was very wrong, and would have pried the reason from me within half an hour. Today they assumed that my misery was all because my aunt had died, and I let them think so.

During assembly and classes and lunch period my friends wrapped me in a protective cocoon of busy-talk. Steff filled me in, in detail, on the sensational entrance Alaiyo had made at the school dance. "In the most absolutely gorgeous raspberry and lavender Senegalese silk robes! And her toenails were painted to match. Alternating colors, I mean. And you should have seen her hair! All the girls were *green*."

"It took me hours to get the corn rows right," Alaiyo added. "With the beads and all. But it was worth it." She gazed dreamily across the lawn to where Asagai was sitting with several members of the soccer team.

It was a gorgeous day, so we were picnicking out of doors, midway between the Cheltenham and Evesham athletic fields. I didn't plan it, I didn't even think about it, but my eyes strayed toward the tree where Greg Barillo and I had eaten lunch the day Aunt Faith had died.

My throat tightened, and I felt guilty being happy about the memory, and then there was Greg himself, wandering over with his crooked grin.

Stephanie gave me a little push. "Go meet him, dodo! You know you want to!"

I didn't know *what* I wanted. But I went.

"How is everything?" Greg asked.

"Like a three-ring circus. You know—'Send in the Clowns' . . ." I checked myself. "Sorry. I didn't mean to dump on you."

"Why not? I'm as good a dumping ground as any," Greg said amiably. He pulled a banana out of his lunchbag, peeled it, then broke it in two and handed me half. "By the way, that test we were going to study for got postponed on account of the jocks in class. They said their practice schedule hadn't allowed them time to study. So maybe we can still cram some tonight."

"Sure, but not tonight. We need some Carlisle family time. For John Henry, you know," I said, and Greg nodded.

"Maybe tomorrow, or the night after?" he asked.

"Okay."

It wasn't till he'd turned back to Cheltenham that I realized I was automatically using the familiar phrases. *Carlisle this* and *Carlisle that*. Being a Carlisle was a part of me.

It could not be true. That letter had to be a joke or some horrible mistake. But Aunt Faith would not, *could* not, have given it to me in that case.

Suddenly, walking back toward Evesham as the late bell for afternoon classes rang, I laughed aloud. *Dad* would know. I was an idiot not to have gone straight to him last night, no matter what the hour. Dad would not have minded being waked up. He would have had a logical explanation, the way he always did.

I went through afternoon classes with a song in my heart.

Then school let out, and I rode home on the bus with my sisters and my brother and my cousin, and everybody was keyed up, acting just a little too normal. Scott, if Mother approved, was going to take John Henry into D.C. on the subway to buy school uniforms. Bruce met us on King Street in his old Chevy, and Tracy went off with him to who-knew-where. Suzi and the older jocks who hang around the video store eyed one another, just as always. We turned down our side street, and there was Featherstone watching for us from the front stoop. Our front door stood open, and the rear one too, the scent of autumn flowers drifting into the house from the back garden.

Mother was in her study, hammering out copy. She looked up briefly. "I thought you might bring Steff and Lee Anne—excuse me, Alaiyo—home with you."

"Steff's meeting her mother to go clothes shopping at the mall, and Alaiyo's watching Asagai play soccer. Mom, when's Dad getting home?"

"He is home. He's leaving for Paris in an hour."

I stared at her, appalled. Mother gave a rueful shrug. "You know what Foreign Service careers are like by now! At least it's only Paris, not the Middle East. He'll be home by the weekend. I have to run him out to Dulles Airport, which is why I'm trying to finish this piece to drop off coming home, so excuse me, honey."

Mom turned back to her typewriter and I ran for my parents' bedroom. "Dad, I need to talk to you—"

"Sorry, kitten." Dad was stowing things with the deftness of long practice in a battered suitcase. "It'll have to wait till the weekend. I'd say come along and talk on the way to the airport, but the car's crammed with junk I don't have time to unload."

I didn't want to talk with a time limit anyway. And for reasons I didn't know, I didn't want to talk to Dad about the contents of that box in front of *anyone,* even Mother.

"Okay," I said. "This weekend." I went back downstairs. Dad followed with his suitcase. He and Mother left.

I surveyed the refrigerator and started, very methodically, to assemble dinner. John Henry wasn't going to have the whole household rallying round him after all, but we'd do the best we could.

Scott came out, sized up the situation, and began making one of his specialties—a grasshopper pie.

"What happened to the shopping expedition?" I asked.

"It'll have to wait till tomorrow. I didn't get a chance to ask the folks, and J.H. has *had* it for today anyway." Scott nodded toward the back garden where our cousin was scuffing stones around. "Too bad Uncle Henry had to take off again so fast."

"That's Foreign Service. As if we didn't know."

"Yeah, but it can be lousy on the kids sometimes," Scott said briefly. I hadn't known he, too, felt that way.

I went on mixing barbecue sauce for the spareribs—I thought that cooking out back on the hibachi would be fun for John Henry—and mentally having an argument with myself about whether to call Greg and invite him over. He was Scott's friend, wasn't he? He liked to cook—Caroline had said so. He would give John Henry some more male companionship. And he, too, had lost a parent when he was young.

I knew I was rationalizing, but was about to yield to temptation anyway when two things occurred simultaneously. The telephone and the doorbell both rang. Scott got the phone as I headed for the door.

I don't know who I expected to see on the doorstep, but it certainly was not Paulina.

She wasn't standing there really. It was more as if she were draped against the doorjamb, with a little help from the wrought-iron railing. She looked at me with heartbroken turquoise eyes.

"Oh. Jessamyn. Where's your mother, dear? I have to see your mother."

I steeled myself. "Mom's driving Dad to Dulles. And she's going into D.C. on her way home, so she won't be back for a while. I'm sorry, Mrs. Payne."

The last thing John Henry needed—the last thing *I* needed—was Paulina weeping in our living room. But Paulina sort of oozed past me before I could prevent it. She made it to the living room sofa before collapsing.

"I'll wait," she said firmly. "Jess, dear, do you think you could manage to find me a little drink? I feel very faint."

"Jess!" Scott bellowed. "Step on it! Didn't you hear me say the call's for you?"

"I'll take it as soon as I can," I said through gritted teeth, and Scott got the message and came to my rescue. I heard him suggesting black coffee, in soothing tones, as I bolted for the kitchen phone.

The caller was Stephanie, nearly hysterical. "I was in Bloomingdale's trying on pants, and when I came out of the dressing room Mother had wandered off. That was an hour ago! I just checked the parking lot, and the car's gone—"

"It's okay, Steff," I told her. "She's here. Scott's coping with her. You'd better get over here fast."

"How?"

"Call a taxi," I said irritably.

Mother arrived just as Steff's taxi pulled up. By then Scott had gotten two cups of black coffee into Paulina, and she had switched from being suicidal to being angry. I couldn't tell whom she was mad at, Stephanie or one of the ex-husbands, but Steff wasn't taking any chances and took refuge in the kitchen.

Mother rolled her eyes at me and started murmuring brightly about what a shame it was that "our dear friend Ali" wasn't going to be coming to the States this autumn after all. "He's an old sheikh's eldest son. Although I don't know whether we'd dare let him meet you, because he has a fatal weakness for sophisticated blondes."

Paulina was an unlovely mess at the moment, but she brightened up considerably at that comment. I went to the kitchen to tell Steff that everything was all right again.

I thawed some more spareribs in the microwave. The Paynes were staying for dinner, that was for sure. Mother wouldn't let them leave till she was convinced Paulina was capable of driving. Suzi came down to see what all the commotion was about, and then Tracy returned with not just Bruce but Greg as well. Greg started showing John Henry how to cook the ribs on the hibachi.

"You guys had better stay too," I said, being elaborately casual.

So Greg called his mother, and then *she* came over. We all ate spareribs and roasted corn and potato salad out in the back garden. I think we were a little slaphappy.

And so help me God, I really, actually, did forget about everything else—*everything*—until once again, very late, I went upstairs to my own room.

And there, like a silent reproach, sat the inlaid box, guarding its secrets in the middle of *not* my great-grandmother Carlisle's Star of Bethlehem quilt.

FIVE

THAT WAS the beginning of a very weird week. I went through all the ordinary September activities like a sleepwalker. No, not like a sleepwalker. As if I were stoned. I've never been stoned, but I've seen some of Suzi's friends enough to know what it's like. I wasn't thinking or feeling, any more than I could help.

I went to Bloomingdale's with Stephanie and approved the pants she'd been trying on. We both went to Cheltenham's soccer game, and lent Alaiyo moral support when Asagai was knocked out briefly. I told Stephanie that she did not have a great moral duty to be her mother's keeper, and

43

that if Paulina were my mother, *I* certainly wouldn't, and what was more, I didn't plan to hold Paulina *or* Steff up through any more crying jags, because they both needed professional counseling, and it was time they faced it.

At this Stephanie, her eyes enormous, gave a carbon copy of her mother's martyred-queen performance and marched off with her head high while Alaiyo turned on me.

"I know how special your aunt was to you, and I know you're entitled to be weird for a while, but you're pushing the outer limits. Don't you think Stephanie has enough trauma to deal with without taking yours on too?"

I glared at Alaiyo, furious, and her eyes softened. "Look, girl, I know it's none of my business, but—"

"You're right. It *is* none of your business. And don't call me *girl*," I retorted irritably. "If I called you girl, you'd belt me."

"That's different," Alaiyo said loftily. She gave me a long look. "I may belt you anyway if you don't wise up." She turned on her heel, leaving me dumbfounded.

All this took place in the parking lot in front of school before a fascinated Cheltenham-Evesham audience waiting to take their buses home.

Tracy saw me and came over. "Beat it. Please," I said through gritted teeth.

"Bruce is coming for me. If you want a ride—"

"No. Thanks. I'll take the late bus." I didn't want to go home just then. I went off, not toward what I now thought of as "our" tree, but toward the meadows out by the corrals. Three of the Cheltenham horses were galloping there, two mares and one of last spring's colts.

For a minute, vividly, I saw Silver, galloping out at Carlisle's Hope.

I shut my eyes.

Behind me a matter-of-fact voice said, "Pretty, isn't she? The little filly. What do you bet she's going to be a good jumper?"

It was Greg, of course. "I don't know," I said in a muffled voice. "I'm not up on horses."

"Yeah, it's your aunt who was the horse person, wasn't she?" he asked, just as matter-of-factly. Thank God for somebody who wasn't bolting away from the subject of Aunt Faith like a frightened steer. "Think your cousin's going to be a horseman?"

"He may be. It's too soon to tell. But his father was on the U.S. equestrian team when he was regular Army. I remember seeing him ride when we lived in Beirut."

"That must have been neat. Did you get to see much of the Arab horses? I hear they're great."

"They are. Aunt Faith used to call them 'grace in motion.'" All at once there I was, in the middle

45

of a perfectly normal conversation, talking about things I'd thought I never could talk about again, and I could hardly believe my ears.

I didn't analyze. I just turned around and grinned at Greg, and he grinned back.

"Been rough, huh?"

"You said it."

"Tune 'em out," Greg advised me. "That's what I did, when I was John Henry's age." I did some mental arithmetic, and realized he must have been about ten, or a year older, when his father died. And as for bolts from the blue, Aunt Faith's accident hadn't held a candle to Mr. Barillo's death. He had keeled over from a massive stroke, right in front of Greg at the breakfast table, while they were on a trip. I began to feel ashamed of myself for the way I'd been behaving.

We scrambled onto the corral fence and smiled at each other again.

"How would you feel if you found out you didn't know who half your family was after all?" This certainly was my day for coming out with things I had not intended saying.

"I *don't* know who they are," Greg said. "Not really. What are you thinking about—that creative writing assignment for Eagleton?"

"Sort of. What do you mean, you don't know?"

Greg shrugged. "All my dad's relatives are back in Italy. He always meant for us to look them up some day, but we never did. And my mom's father walked out when she was eleven. He was 'a travelin' man with wanderlust in his legs and a soul made o' blarney,'" Greg said in an Irish brogue that made me giggle. "Gram was so mad at the whole O'Rourke family, she wouldn't let Mom or my uncle have anything to do with any of them after that. You remember what my Gram was like," he added meaningfully. I did indeed.

"Doesn't it bother you, not knowing?"

Greg looked surprised. "I know who *I* am. Actually I kind of feel like it makes our family tree more interesting. Like there's a mystery waiting to be solved someday."

It hadn't occurred to me to look at it like that.

I slid down from the fence. "Thanks. I guess I'd better go or I'll miss the late bus."

"You have loads of time still." Greg hesitated. "What about studying for that test tonight? You want to?"

"I've got—things to do tonight. How about tomorrow?" Tomorrow was Friday. It dawned on me that I sounded as if I were fishing for a date, and I blushed.

"Maybe we could go bowling or something. After we study, of course." Greg slid down too. Then he said good-bye and left me feeling discombobulated from all the new ideas that were whirling through my head.

I went home and found that Dad had called to

say he would not be home till Sunday night. That did not upset me as it would have a few hours earlier. Everybody else was home, busy with preparations for another cookout in the garden.

Suzi looked up at me and raised an eyebrow. "Well!" she said with meaning. "It's nice to see that the Wicked Witch of the West has finally taken a leave of absence."

"Shut up," I said mildly, and checked out the refrigerator for salad makings. But before I started on the salad, I went to my room, shut the door, and made two telephone calls. One was to Stephanie, the other was to Alaiyo. Both were apologies.

The inlaid box was sitting on my bureau. I gave it a pat before I went back downstairs.

Dinner was relatively peaceful—peaceful for our house, that is. Mother looked around the garden and affected dramatic astonishment. "I can't believe it! Nobody here but us family!"

"*I'm* here," John Henry said.

"I *said* family," Mother answered.

For once we got to bed at a decent hour. Nobody complained when Mother switched the TV off firmly before it was even nine o'clock. "I vote we all take advantage of the night off while we have it. Sometimes I think we're operating a combination airline terminal, hotel, and nuthouse." She covered her typewriter, swiped her new library book out of Tracy's hands, and departed for the master bedroom.

- I went upstairs too, my heart thumping. It was time to do what I'd been putting off.

But first I took a bubble bath. Then I washed my hair so I wouldn't have to do it in the morning. I had to throw Featherstone out twice—once from the bathroom, where he was trying to eat the bubbles, and once from my bedroom, where he was happily gnawing on my new Adidas. At last I got into bed beneath the Star of Bethlehem quilt. Me and the inlaid box.

I wasn't going to chicken out this time, and I was going to be businesslike and organized. I even had a notebook and a pen to list the contents.

There weren't that many, just the letter I'd read, the other letters I hadn't looked at yet, that photograph of Great-grandmother Faith, and another photograph, from the same photographer, of a man in side whiskers whom I didn't recognize. Douglas Carlisle?

Slid down to one side was a wad of tissue paper. I opened it, perhaps unconsciously postponing facing those other letters. A heavy gold ring rolled out. It was plain, with initials inside.

W. C. E. *to* F. D. E.

F. D. Faith Dryden? I knew those were Great-grandmother Faith's maiden initials; they were embroidered in one corner of the quilt. But what did the *E.* stand for? And who was W. C. E.?

I moved on to the envelopes. There was a fat one, with a return address that read *Selective Service—Official Business.*

Selective Service? Wasn't that what they used to call the military draft? The memory came vaguely from a twentieth-century history class. The envelope bore no postmark, and it was addressed to *Local Board No. 1* in a county in New Jersey. (New Jersey? Had any of the family ever lived there? I was beginning to feel like a detective spotting clues.)

Inside were other envelopes. A battered one from Pittsburgh was addressed to my grandfather, with the address of the Allegheny County Courthouse scribbled on the back in pencil. Inside was a brief letter.

TRINITY EVANGELICAL AND REFORMED CHURCH
E. ROY CORMAN, PASTOR
WILKINSBURG, PA.

October 26, 1942

To Whom It May Concern:

According to our church records William Charles Edwards was baptized November 12, 1899, by the Rev. C. L. Alspach, then pastor of Trinity.

Sincerely,
E. Roy Corman

William Charles Edwards? I plowed doggedly on.

The next envelope bore the New York Telephone Company's Willoughby Street, Brooklyn, return imprint, but no mailing address. Only a notation in an angular hand: *Carbons of letters*.

I took the first one out, yellow onionskin, wartime brittle. It was dated November 19, 1942.

MEMO TO MR. J. P. ANDREWS:

I am submitting herewith a certified copy of my birth record as evidence of my United States citizenship in accordance with your memorandum of 9/15/42 to all employees required by the government to have FBI security clearance.

This certificate, however, bears the surname Edwards, which appears on the company records as my middle name, Edward. In tracing my birth records, I find that my mother married my stepfather, Douglas Scott Carlisle, in 1906. About two years later the family moved to New York City, at which time I was entered in the New York City schools under the surname Carlisle. I have used this name ever since, and my marriage and children's births are recorded under this name.

I have been unable to find any evidence that my stepfather formally adopted me in order to legalize my use of his name.

Having in mind the complications the family may at some time encounter, as well as the present security clearance requirements, it seems advisable for me to obtain the legal right to use my present surname. In this connection I will appreciate any advice or assistance you can give me as to the procedure to be followed to accomplish this. I should also appreciate your advice as to whether any further data or affidavits are required for the company's records.

I sat up straight, my heart pounding.

My grandfather, Charles Edward Carlisle, was not a Carlisle, but he *was* the son of Great-grandmother Faith Dryden Carlisle. And of someone else. W.C.E. W. C. Edwards. When had that first husband, my real great-grandfather, died? Why had the *Carlisle*, not the *Edwards*, heritage been passed on to us as a touchstone to live by? Come to think of it, why didn't I know anything about the Drydens?

And another fascinating little item. My grandfather had needed FBI security clearance. Why? And had he ever gotten it? Then the timing of the letter struck me. 1942, when America was in the grip of World War II—

Greg had been right: There was a mystery waiting to be solved. And it *did* make the family tree more interesting.

I snapped out the light and slid down beneath the Star of Bethlehem quilt that had belonged to a blood-kin great-grandmother after all. Something warm and heavy landed with a plop beside me. Featherstone, settling himself with a half sigh, half groan. His arrival pushed a smooth, hard object against my hand. Aunt Faith's box. Pandora's box. A myriad of tantalizing questions and possibilities were jostling each other in my brain. I could almost see Aunt Faith giving me a Mona Lisa smile, and for the first time since that awful Wednesday I was able to think of her without pain.

Six

The next day was Friday. I wished desperately that it was Sunday. It was going to be very difficult going through a day of school without spilling the beans about the inlaid box to Stephanie and Alaiyo, not to mention Greg. Especially Greg. I had a pretty good idea that if I were going to start digging up family skeletons, my father would not appreciate my going public before I talked to him. And I was determined to do that digging. If I wasn't blood-Carlisle, I wanted to know *who* I was, and the mere name Edwards was not enough.

Fortunately Dad was arriving home some time on Sunday. Until then I would have to keep my mouth shut as best I could. It wasn't hard at home, because breakfast time around our house is crazy. And when I reached school, I had other traumas to occupy my mind. Stephanie was waiting at our lockers, and she looked half sick.

"What happened?" I demanded, immediately forgetting my resolve to stop minding other people's business.

"My father called last night. He wants me to come visit him. Over Columbus Day. For a week."

"Which father?" I asked practically.

"My real one," Stephanie said starkly, and I gasped.

Alaiyo, reaching us at this moment, gave a low whistle. "Steff, you haven't heard from him in years."

"I know it. Not since Mother let him off the child-support hook after she married The Pain." She meant the latest stepfather, Mr. Payne. Out of her mother's presence Stephanie never referred to her stepfathers except by sarcastic nicknames. "Needless to say, she's been trying to get her hooks into him again for the past six months. I never thought he'd let himself be found, let alone call *her!* But he did. He wants to see me."

The warning bell rang at this interesting point, and we moved out into the hall. "I should think you'd be glad," I said in a whisper. "He *is* your own father."

Steff just gave me a look. "We lived together

for exactly three and a half years. The last letter I got from him was three years ago. The last present was the year before that, and it was a doll. When I was *eleven!*"

"A two-hundred-dollar music-box collectors' doll," Alaiyo put in dryly.

"That's not the point. The point is, there's a dance at Cheltenham on Columbus Day. Have you forgotten? And I want to be at it, not at whatever godforsaken place my dear deserting father's chosen to hole up in now!"

"I thought it was your mother who walked out of that marriage. And the place can't be too godforsaken if he could telephone."

"Don't be so technical," Stephanie retorted irritably. "The point is, I've made plans for that weekend, and nobody cares that I don't want to change them."

But Steff doesn't have a date for the dance yet, a voice in my head said. She hardly ever has a date. She doesn't give boys a chance.

"I wouldn't worry too much," Alaiyo said, getting back to the subject of the visit. "Ten to one your mother won't let you go."

"Yes, she will, if she gets a fat check from my father first. They had an awful fight. I'm sick of being a pawn!" Stephanie said violently.

"That's not the point either, is it?" I said abruptly. Passersby turned curiously, and I lowered my voice. "You don't want to see him. You really don't want to see him. You're afraid to, aren't you? Steff, *why?*"

"Wouldn't you be?" Stephanie demanded. "He's my flesh and blood, but he's—a stranger. I might as well have been adopted as a baby. I wish I had been. Oh, you wouldn't understand!"

Oh, wouldn't I, I thought, watching her sweep into math class. Poor Stephanie. Maybe it was better not to know who your ancestors were than to know *about* the significant ones only not really know them.

My thoughts were getting tangled, and I settled down to English class with something like relief.

While Eagleton droned on about our research papers, my mind drifted to Greg . . . to the conversation I'd had with him yesterday by the corral. And that was when I got my big idea.

I would do my research paper on Mr. W. C. Edwards, who happened to be my great-grandfather, but whom I didn't know a thing about, other than that he was dead by 1906.

I was so engrossed in this date that I literally bumped into Greg at lunchtime without seeing him, right in the middle of the outdoor commons. My books went flying, I turned red, and a lot of people turned to stare. Greg didn't seem to mind. In fact, he barely noticed, and I admired his cool.

"I was coming to look for you," he said. "Are we still on for tonight? For studying, I mean," he added, apparently thinking I'd forgotten.

I wondered what on earth my face was communicating, and quickly put on what I hoped was an airy smile. "Oh, yes. Definitely!" I said glibly, and went to find Suzi to bribe her to let me have the family room to myself that night.

"I would have anyway," Suzi said after driving a hard bargain. "This is the first thing that's had you acting halfway human since—" She stopped. "Don't worry," she said briskly. "I'll see that John Henry and Scott clear out too." Tracy, we knew, didn't have to be considered; she was sure to be otherwise engaged.

Since we are, as Mother grandly puts it, "without staff at the moment"—meaning, she hasn't found a new cleaning woman since the last one quit—I spent the afternoon making the family room shine. It's really a great place, an addition tacked on behind the kitchen, which Mother had had remodeled into what a Colonial kitchen would have looked like if the colonists had had gas, electricity, freezers, built-in ovens, microwaves, and computers. The only trouble is that the two rooms are almost totally open to each other, which makes privacy impossible without negotiation.

Mother, coming in on my labors, inquired about the sudden concern for neatness and just said "hmm" when she heard the reason. Scott was more blunt.

"Greg's a good kid. And a friend of mine."

"So?"

"So don't dump on him like you've been doing to the rest of us. He doesn't need it."

"For your information we're going to study. And possibly go bowling," I said coldly. "And since you were not exactly uninvolved in the mess in here, it wouldn't hurt you to pitch in a little."

Scott did so without comment, other than to mention casually that he was taking John Henry to a movie after dinner. Actually nobody said much, for which I was profoundly grateful. It was crazy, but as seven-thirty approached, my heart began pounding. Then the bell rang. I opened the door, and at the sight of Greg's familiar grin everything settled back to usual.

No, not quite usual. The family was discreetly absent, except for Featherstone, who assumed he was the main attraction. Greg scratched his stomach and pulled his ears, and we settled down on the couch with *Great Expectations* while the scents and sounds of the Virginia twilight came through the open door from the back garden. I could have purred.

Greg turned out to like Dickens as much as my father does. I do *not* like Dickens, so it was a big help to hear an analysis of the story from Greg's point of view. It was also a considerable jolt. Maybe because I'd loathed having to read it, I had done so in a couple of all-nighters two weeks ago and almost nothing had registered on my consciousness. It did now.

"The main characters, Pip and Estella," Greg explained, "are both orphans. They know very little of the truth about their history. They're both raised to have great expectations that are unwarranted and to believe as gospel things that are—"

"A pack of lies!" I said vehemently, and then felt hot.

Greg raised his eyebrows. "Not lies really. It was more distortions of truth. Or fibs to make everyone feel better."

"What's the difference if it meant they were raised to put faith in things that weren't real? And how good can somebody feel when she—he—finds out he's lived his whole life on a false premise? Not to mention false values?"

"Everybody runs into that some time or another, doesn't he? And whether any given value is true or false is pretty subjective." Greg's eyes were twinkling. "Which, as if you didn't know, is not going to make you popular with Eagleton. On the test you'd better stick to writing only what you can back up with hard data."

I'd heard that before. "You sound like Mom's editor," I grumbled.

The magical mood had been broken.

Greg looked at me and closed his book. "Why don't we take a break?" he suggested. "Want to walk over to King Street and get a Coke or something?"

I noticed he didn't say anything about bowling. Not that I like bowling so much. I just had an uneasy feeling that I'd blown it.

I called up to Mother, who was in her study "thinking out a story"—meaning, watching television—that we were going over to the main drag, and we let ourselves out into the velvet night.

One of the nice things about living in Old Town is that you're so close to things. A couple of blocks along cobbled, lamplit streets, and we were strolling down toward the river, past quaint brick storefronts. Tourists were ambling along, hand in hand. Jazz floated from one upstairs window, and folk guitar from another. Old Town is full of coffeehouses, restaurants, gourmet-food places, boutiques, and pubs.

We saw Tracy and Bruce across the street, in line for one of the music hangouts. They waved and we waved back. "How about here?" Greg asked, nodding toward a coffeehouse we were passing. Metal tables and chairs were set out in a tree-filled atrium. There weren't many people, and we found a quiet table in the back. Greg went to the counter and brought back our orders: pastries, espresso for him, and Capuccino—heavy on the milk—for me.

"That book's really getting to you, isn't it?" he asked.

"What?"

"*Great Expectations*. Or is it your aunt, or the combination?" It was like Greg to come right out with something without worrying endlessly about how the question might make me feel.

I countered just as directly. "How did it make you feel to have to deal with your father's suddenly not being there? Not just him, but—financially and everything? You weren't much older than John Henry." *And my grandfather*, I thought, *had been even younger*. "Were you scared?"

Greg didn't take offense. "Only for a day or so. Then I knew we'd be okay. And I started realizing how much I'd gotten from him while he was alive. I'm still realizing."

"How would you feel if your mother got married again?"

"I wish she would," Greg said. "If she married somebody who'd make her happy. If you're asking me how I'd feel about her marrying Nick Buyukas, that's something else."

"He seems to make her happy."

"Half the time. The other half he makes her miserable or absolutely furious."

"Does he want to get married?"

It was weird; Greg and I seemed to be able to say anything to each other.

"He wants to marry her," Greg said. "I mean,

he wants *her*. He's not so keen on the rest of us. He doesn't see why a couple needs family around. He's not used to tight family units like you and I have."

Something in my face must have changed.

Greg reached for his espresso. "Anyway," he said lightly, "I wouldn't talk about remarriage around John Henry yet. The kid's not ready for it."

"I wasn't thinking of John Henry."

Alaiyo would have said, *"Ohhh?"* But Greg just sat there and sipped espresso. And in another five minutes I'd done exactly what I'd vowed I wouldn't do. I'd told him the whole story—as I knew it so far—about my great-grandmother and her marriages.

I had a strong suspicion my own parents would kill me when they found out, but it was worth it.

SEVEN

Dad came home Sunday and he didn't kill me. His reaction to the box of papers was even more surprising.

But I'm getting ahead of myself. The result of my talk with Greg was these conclusions:

1. Families were incomprehensible, exasperating, but important;
2. The unfolding saga of my great-grandparents would make a fascinating research paper;
3. To make that paper acceptable to Eagleton would demand a lot of work;

4. Greg would be delighted to help me with the research.

I floated home from the coffeehouse on a pink cloud, and I did not tell my family what we'd been discussing. Suzi took one look at me and assumed that it had not been *Great Expectations*. "It wasn't a discussion either, was it?" she inquired upstairs later.

"Wouldn't you love to know?" I said tantalizingly, and Suzi said, "*Great Expectations*, hmm," with meaning.

I threw something at her and sailed out of the bathroom, my exit marred by Featherstone, who was standing on the hem of my quilted robe.

On Saturday the rest of my family nobly restrained themselves from asking about my date. On Sunday we had Scott's pecan waffles for breakfast and went to church, where we saw the Websters. Alaiyo had no such noble inhibitions. I told her only that Greg and I had studied, had gone out for coffee, and had had a very good time. I left everything else out. With Alaiyo this was partly self-defense. Having teased her about her own Search-for-Ancestors kick, I was not about to let her get back at me now.

At the lunch table Mother, thinking that keeping busy was John Henry's best antidote for brooding, announced that we were going on an expedition to Mount Vernon. "Just us," she said, casting one eye at Tracy and the other at the phone. So Tracy didn't bring up Bruce and I didn't bring up Greg. We packed a picnic basket and tried to get on the road before any calls came from Paulina.

We were just starting out the door when the phone rang. "Don't answer it!" Scott shouted.

Mother frowned. "It could be your father."

I hoped not; that would mean he would not be home that night. But it wasn't Dad, or Paulina either; it was Greg, suggesting we get together again to study *Great Expectations*. I explained what we were up to, and hung up quickly as Scott honked the horn.

Since it was September, there weren't too many tourists at Mount Vernon. I've seen it a dozen times, but I always love it. We realized quickly, however, that bringing John Henry had not been the best idea in the world. There was a horse in the pasture that looked a lot like Silver, and John Henry got that solemn, old-man quietness again. Mother and I looked at each other, and Mother sighed. "I *wish* Henry were here," she said for the umpteenth time.

"That's the Foreign Service for you," I said with an edge to my voice. Mother's eyes narrowed.

"Jessamyn, I am getting a little tired of hearing your prejudices on that subject," she said quietly. "It would be refreshing if just once you could say something about the advantages you've received from being a Foreign Service brat. If you'd grown up at Carlisle's Hope, you'd probably be complaining about having been stuck in one place all your life."

I was genuinely startled—for a lot of reasons. I slunk off and suggested to John Henry that we pay a visit to the Mount Vernon kitchen, which is one of my favorite places, and we did. Then we made a grand tour of the grounds, and Scott started talking about one of his fantasies; which was to stage a sound and light show at Mount Vernon during the summer season. He got carried away, as usual, but he got John Henry carried away with him. Pretty soon they were deep in technical plans, and I plopped down in one of the gardens, glad for some solitude, and contemplated my life and state of mind.

The word for it, I had to confess, was *confused*.

Before I could get depressed, I went looking for my family and found that they'd staked out a picnic site, and that our number had grown to seven.

"Look who happened to turn up," Mother said dryly, indicating Greg. I blushed. Greg held up his camera and said he'd biked out, thinking he and Scott and John Henry might try some time exposures of sunset over the Potomac. Scott and John

Henry thought that was a great idea, so the upshot was, I didn't get much out of having Greg there anyway.

"I thought I said just family," Mother said to me after Greg had gone off with Scott and John Henry.

"Didn't it work out well that he decided on his own to come out here?" I asked just as innocently. Clearly John Henry was enjoying having Greg around.

We got home around nine, and the house was lit up, and Dad was there. There was the usual hubbub of catching up on the week's happenings, his and ours, but when the kitchen emptied out, Dad turned to me.

"You wanted to talk to me about something. Still want to?"

"I want to show you something." I ran upstairs and brought back the inlaid box, shutting the kitchen door behind me. Dad's eyebrows rose.

"Like that, is it? Secret and confidential?" Then he saw what I held, and an interested, nostalgic expression spread across his face. "Wherever did that surface? I haven't seen it in years."

"You know what it is?"

"Sure, I know it. It used to stand on Dad's chest of drawers and hold his watch and things. I haven't seen it since he died. Where did you find it?"

68

"Uncle Henry gave it to me. He said Aunt Faith found it in the attic at Carlisle's Hope and wanted me to have it."

I stood, rigid, as Dad took his coffee and the box to the kitchen table, sat down, and lifted the lid. "Looks like a lot of old letters," he commented. "Have you read them?"

"Yes."

Maybe something in my monosyllable got through to him. He looked at me, then turned and devoted himself to the papers.

And that was when I got the jolt.

He opened the first paper, the one about there being no record of adoption, and he didn't turn a hair. He went on to the one about the FBI, and his face took on a look I knew well—interested, curious, amused.

"I had no idea Dad had so much trouble getting security clearance."

You knew about it?

"Sure. I found out when I was being cleared for overseas posting." Dad looked at the date on the paper. "Nineteen forty-two. I was only eight. That's probably why he didn't talk about it at home."

"I don't mean about the FBI! Did you know your father wasn't Douglas Scott Carlisle's son?"

"Everyone knew it. It wasn't a secret." Dad sounded faintly astonished. "He dropped the William and added the Carlisle because he was always called Charles anyway, and he was very fond of Douglas Carlisle."

"I *didn't* know," I said tightly. Dad looked up, alert, and I raced on. "I don't think any of us knows we're not really Carlisles. Ever since we were born, you've been stuffing us with the Carlisle heritage, you and Mom. It's what's supposed to make up for us being dragged all over the globe with no roots of our own, and all the time it was a big lie, because we *aren't* Carlisles. You deliberately deceived us—"

"Hold on a minute." Something in Dad's voice brought me up short. "First of all," he went on gently, "it was no secret. If Gadge and Aunt Meg and your mother and I never talked about it, it's because we just took it for granted. I know my father did. Second of all, what's the big deal?"

"We aren't Carlisles. We believed in all the—the standards, the banner and the war cry and everything. And they're not ours. Doesn't that *bother* you?"

"Why should it?" my father asked reasonably. "I know who *I* am. I'm Douglas Edward Carlisle."

"How can you be?"

Dad laughed and reached in his pocket for his passport. "For the best reason in the world. The U.S. Government says I am. And your passport says Jessamyn Faith Carlisle. Your *diplomatic* passport," he emphasized, "so you can be quite sure you have a right to the Carlisle name."

"Even if Grandfather was never officially adopted?"

"Even if. My birth certificate says Carlisle, our marriage license says Carlisle, *your* birth certificates say Carlisle. You know why I didn't have any difficulty proving my right to the name when I got my government clearance? Because my father had had security clearance as Charles Edward Carlisle."

Then he'd gotten the proof he'd needed for the FBI. I wondered how.

"So," Dad concluded, "there's no reason for you to have qualms about claiming the Carlisle banner and all the rest. Including the roots." He looked at me. "Except you do have qualms, don't you?"

I nodded. Dad pushed the chair across from him out from under the table with his toe. "Why don't you get yourself some coffee and cake and sit down? You look like you could use it."

I obeyed.

"Has it really bothered you as much as all that?" Dad asked. "Being a Foreign Service brat? Your mother and I wondered once or twice whether we should have left you with your grandmother or your aunt when we went to hardship posts."

"It hasn't bothered the others," I answered honestly. "And being left behind while the two of you went without us would have been the pits! I

71

just . . . wish I could have grown up in one place—all of us together, in my own country, like everybody else does." I conveniently overlooked the number of families I knew who were like ours—or worse, like Stephanie's. "I wish I could have grown up belonging to Carlisle's Hope."

"You do belong to it," Dad said gently. "All of you do, but you especially. Even your uncle said that last weekend." He smiled slightly. "Jess, I do understand your feelings about being a service brat. I guess that's why I stressed the Carlisle heritage so much—as you said—to give you roots to fall back on. The way I did when I became the man of the family after my father died. The way *he* did when his mother and stepfather were married. He got a big thrill out of the idea his mother wasn't just marrying a man—she was marrying a whole clan! That's why he wanted to change his name to Carlisle."

"Then why wasn't there an adoption or a legal name change?" Something else occurred to me. "Why haven't we ever known any Carlisle relatives other than Aunt Meg and Aunt Faith and Uncle Charlie?" (Uncle Charlie was Dad's younger brother who'd been killed in Vietnam.) "For that matter, why haven't we ever known any Dryden or Edwards relatives? I'd never even heard of them."

"I don't know why, except that apparently your great-grandmother lost touch with the Pittsburgh connections after she moved to New York.

The world wasn't as small, you know, in 1908 as it is now. And as for the adoption business, I suppose they never thought it was necessary. Dad *felt* like a Carlisle. He felt that Douglas Scott Carlisle was his father. He *chose* to be a Carlisle. Don't you think something you deliberately choose is often more yours than something you've just inherited with no say in the matter?"

I sipped my coffee, feeling warmth spread through me.

"Anyway, by the time he needed legal documentation, his mother and stepfather were both dead," Dad said. "They were dead by the time he met your grandmother. That's another reason we don't know any other Carlisles. Carlisle's Hope came to my father from a distant cousin who died while I was a kid. And *my* father died without a will, so his estate couldn't be settled till Faith was twenty-one. By that time Gadge wanted to move to Florida, so we put Carlisle's Hope into a trust for Meg and Faith and me. And if you really want to know more about all of this, you ought to ask Gadge."

"Dad, would you mind?" I asked, my face glowing.

"Of course I wouldn't mind. Gadge would certainly know more about this whole business with the FBI in 1942 than I do. Maybe she has some other papers."

"And . . . would you mind if I do some digging into the Dryden and Edwards backgrounds? Would you mind if I wrote a paper for school about it?"

"Of course not."

I kissed him and went upstairs to phone my grandmother.

EIGHT

FORTUNATELY MY grandmother is a night owl. I'd forgotten to check the time before I called her.

"That's all right. I'm watching old cops-and-robbers reruns on TV," she said comfortably. "How are you doing, dear?"

"We're fine. John Henry's hanging in."

"And holding in?"

"You said it." I cast a wary eye at my bedroom door, which I'd closed tightly, and lowered my voice. "Gadge, Uncle Henry gave me an inlaid wood box that used to belong to Grandfather. He said Aunt Faith found it in her attic and wanted me to have it."

I heard Gadge catch her breath. "*That* box. It belonged to Charlie's stepfather. I wondered what had happened to it."

"So had Dad. He said I should call you." I took a deep breath of my own. "Gadge, I never knew before—about Douglas Carlisle not being my grandfather's real father." I hurried on through her disconcerted exclamation. "There are some papers in the box, letters and carbons, about Grandfather trying to establish his I.D. in 1942."

"Good heavens, I'd almost forgotten about that," Gadge said ruefully. Her voice changed. "Jess, are you upset about it?"

"Not anymore. I don't think so. But I'm interested. Anyway, I'm stuck with a research paper for Eagleton"—Gadge had heard all about Eagleton from me last Christmas—"and I sort of thought I'd like to do one on that side of the family."

"And you wondered what I might have available." Gadge chuckled. "My condo doesn't have an attic like Carlisle's Hope, but I'll check my bottom bureau drawer."

Gadge's bottom bureau drawer was legendary—a catchall of souvenirs. A long time ago Tracy and I spent a memorable afternoon rooting through some old love letters we'd found there. Gadge had not been pleased.

Gadge chuckled again, no doubt remembering. "And you could ask your Uncle Henry to have a look around the attic at the farm for you," she suggested.

"He's not coming back from Japan till Christmastime. If then."

"Oh," Gadge said. "Jessamyn, if John Henry needs me, you give me a phone call and I'll catch a plane, you hear?"

"Yes, ma'am," I said fervently, and hung up after being assured that she'd put anything interesting from the bottom drawer in the mail tomorrow.

My comment about none of us knowing that Grandfather was not born a Carlisle must really have registered on Dad. At breakfast the next morning he threw the fact out in his typical offhand way.

"Did you call Gadge?" he asked me, reaching for another English muffin. And as I nodded, he casually added to the others, "Jess is going to do some genealogical research on Dad's real father for a school research paper."

"What do you mean, his *real* father?" Scott and Tracy said at once.

"What do you mean, for a school paper?" Mother demanded, looking at me hard.

I looked anywhere but at people's faces.

"I mean, his own father, William Edwards, your great-grandmother Faith Carlisle's first husband," Dad replied. "Somebody please pass me the jam."

"I don't see why Jess has to go rooting around in family history," Mother said to my astonishment.

"I can think of one good reason," Scott said. "Because there seem to be some pieces of it that we don't know about."

But he didn't look shocked, just interested. Nobody looked the way I'd felt when I first found out the truth.

"I can't get over it," I said to Steff and Alaiyo as we were having lunch. Now that the family knew about the skeleton in the closet, I felt free to talk about it. "Nobody really cared."

Alaiyo shrugged. "Not everybody's interested in ancestors," she remarked pointedly. "And not everybody needs roots as much as you do."

I hadn't known that showed. I looked at the two of them, disconcerted. Stephanie was nodding.

"Anyway," Alaiyo said matter-of-factly, "it doesn't take anything away from you, does it? It just gives you a possibility of some things to add on to your history."

"What about John Henry?" Stephanie asked.

"That's a good question. To have the under-pinnings knocked out from him is something he doesn't need."

"What did he say when this all came out?"

"Nothing. He never says anything. Except with Scott and Greg when they're talking about their hobbies." I considered. "Maybe John Henry could help me with my research. He seems to like being in on things with Greg—"

"Oh, Greg's in on this too," Alaiyo said knowingly.

"Lay off," I retorted. "I'm serious. John Henry's walking around like a zombie, and maybe being in on a detective search for a new great-grandfather would help him belong. He certainly isn't going to see his father for quite a while."

"Speaking of which," Alaiyo said with meaning, and we both looked at Stephanie.

"Don't ask," she said darkly. "Mother's getting letters from lawyers. She's seeing lawyers." She shrugged and said in a brittle voice, "So what else is new?"

"Don't you think you ought to at least *think* about seeing your father?"

"No," Stephanie replied distinctly. "I don't want to dig up family skeletons, and if you have any sense, you won't either. And I won't go visit him; I don't care what happens."

With that Stephanie got up and left the table.

Alaiyo looked at me and rolled her eyes. "Not facing things never made them any better."

I had an uneasy feeling she was talking about me as well as Stephanie.

It was Friday before the result of Gadge's drawer cleaning reached me. In between a lot of things happened.

Eagleton approved my proposal for a family

research paper. "So long as it is really researched," he said snippily. "The purpose of the assignment is to teach you scientific research methods. You'll need proper documentary evidence, footnotes, and a bibliography."

"I'm already working on it," I said coldly. I was planning to attach that letter from the Office of the Prothonotary, whatever that was.

Dad meanwhile was seeing lawyers and making telephone calls to Japan. He was handling all the legal matters of Aunt Faith's estate for Uncle Henry.

"We'll probably have to go out to Carlisle's Hope sometime this fall," he told Mother.

I didn't want to think about going there again with no Aunt Faith to greet me. John Henry just went on with what he was doing as if he hadn't heard.

I got John Henry to say he'd help me with my research. We made a list of all the places we could look for genealogical research—court records, census records, old newspapers. *He* thought Eagleton's research requirements were fascinating.

On Wednesday Stephanie, stiff-lipped, informed us that her father had filed for a court order to let her visit him. "*Let* me! As if I wanted to and was being held back against my will!"

On Thursday Dad and Mother entertained visiting foreign dignitaries. Not at our house this time, thank goodness. Since the dignitaries' arrival in D.C. was without warning, and we had not yet solved the housecleaning problem, Dad phoned Mother to meet them at the Ritz-Carlton's Jockey Club for tea, and they'd take it from there. Mother, congratulating herself for having bought a new raw silk suit, drove in to town.

Half an hour later, while the rest of us were starting to fix hamburgers, the doorbell rang. Scott answered it. "Good grief!" we heard him say in pleased astonishment. "When did *you* roll in?"

We ran to the kitchen doorway to see what was going on. There on our doorstep, a Rolls-Royce in the background, stood "our pal Ali," the Arab prince.

"I did not roll in. I flew in," Ali corrected, heading for the kitchen. "Jessamyn, I cannot believe it, you have turned into a young lady. Tracy, you grow more gorgeous with each passing year." He kissed our hands grandly. "And this can't be Susan!"

"Suzi," my sister said, batting her eyes.

"Knock it off," I told her under my breath.

Ali's eyes were twinkling. "Knock it off, indeed, or I will forget I am your—what do you call it? Your godfather?" He turned to Scott. "Where is Doug? And your glamorous mama? I just got off the plane from London and I do not have any business until Monday so I thought, Aha! I will invite myself to dinner with my very good friends the Carlisles."

Tracy grinned. "You're out of luck, Ali. Mom and Dad are at the Jockey Club. You can catch them there if you want." She mentioned who it was they were entertaining, and Ali made a face.

"My government is not pleased with their government right now. Besides, they are bores." He sniffed the kitchen appreciatively.

Scott laughed. "If you want to settle for Carlisleburgers, I guess we can let you."

If not quite our godfather, Ali's the closest thing to it a Muslim can be to Presbyterians, and he took the responsibility very seriously. Suzi and Tracy and I were completely safe with him, which is more than I could say for anyone else in skirts between the ages of fifteen and fifty-five. Ali has, shall we say, an international "reputation," which our parents are hopeful we don't know about. He's not just a colleague of Dad's, but a dear family friend.

Ali ended up joining us around the kitchen table. We were halfway through dinner when the doorbell rang again. This time I answered it. This time it was Paulina.

Only it was Paulina as I hadn't seen her for a long time. She was wearing a sapphire-blue suit, her lipstick was on straight, and she was cold sober. She looked fabulous—and she was filled with fury.

"I'm going to sue that rat!" she fumed. "I'm

going to take him for every cent he has!" Whether she was referring to Stephanie's father or her latest husband, I had no idea. "Jess—would you believe it?—I came out of the lawyer's and drove two blocks and the bloody car broke down again." I could believe it. The Payne car broke down regularly because Paulina always forgot to have it serviced. "And of course, all the garages are closed for the night by now, so maybe one of you could run me home, or I can call from here for a cab—" Her blue eyes widened. "*Ohhhh!*" she said, her voice rising and falling like a Siamese cat's.

I didn't have to turn around to know what had happened. Ali had emerged from the kitchen and was standing behind me.

I mentally crossed all my fingers. "Mrs. Payne, may I present Prince Ali Youssef."

Neither of them wasted any time. In two shakes Ali was in front of me, bending to kiss her hand, and Paulina's hand was under his nose before he'd reached for it. "I've heard about you," Paulina said, in a voice that showed me where Suzi'd gotten those throaty tones she used when trying to sound sexy.

"And I could not have heard of you, dear lady," Ali responded gallantly, "because you would have been impossible to forget." I heard Scott groan. Fortunately Paulina and Ali didn't; they were too busy. Ali was offering to drive her

83

wherever she was going, and murmuring about his Rolls, and in two minutes they had swept out on a cloud of Paulina's expensive French perfume.

"Open the windows and air the place out," Tracy said when they'd gone. Scott shook his head, John Henry looked baffled, and I phoned Stephanie to tell her not to expect her mother for a while.

"I just hope she doesn't get any ideas," Stephanie said philosophically.

"I hope *he* doesn't."

"At least it would take her mind off my father and The Pain."

I found out in school on Friday that Ali had not delivered Paulina to her doorstep until two a.m. I called Mother at lunchtime to tell her that, and Mother groaned. "I'd better have a talk with Ali," she said. "The last thing Paulina needs right now is to be loved and left."

"I thought she might be at the house telling you all about it."

"She's probably just getting up now. Maybe I'd better have a talk with her too. See you, love," Mother said, and hung up.

I'm afraid I didn't give much thought to Ali and Paulina, because Greg and I spent lunchtime planning a trip to the Library of Congress for genealogical research.

When I reached home after school, Paulina was there, and so was a fat envelope from my grandmother. I looked at it, feeling slightly shaky.

"Aren't you going to open it?" Suzi asked.

"Not right now." I didn't want an audience. I stuck it in my knapsack, left the house unnoticed, and wandered over to the only place I could think of where I was unlikely to run into anyone I knew—the enclosed churchyard behind the old brick church. I sat down on a stone bench and opened the packet.

A note was enclosed, on one of my grandmother's violet-spattered note sheets.

Jess, dear,
    Hope this is useful. You can keep them if you like.

                  Love,
                  Gadge

Inside were some more envelopes, postmarked Pittsburgh, Pennsylvania.

Oct. 7, 1942

Dear Charles,

    In the first place I am glad to hear from you, and would like to know more about your life. I remember you as a baby, here in Pittsburgh, and later as a lad, when you were living with your mother in an apartment in N.Y. City.

    Your mother was my father's niece, the daughter of my father's sister, Aunt Sis. My father, Dr. W. F. Edmundson, died in 1931. I knew your mother well. I also knew Mr. Edwards. Of course, I knew Uncle Jimmy and Clarence Dryden well. I don't believe I ever met Mr. Carlisle, your stepfather, during any of my trips to N.Y. City. I was mostly at the farm, Carlisle's Hope, while he was away on business.

I remember when you were born—but, of course, cannot recall the date. You were born on Bennett Street, located in the Homewood District of Pgh. At that time Homewood was a district of fields, with an occasional pond, and mud streets, and rather sparsely populated. The event is firmly impressed on my mind because my aunt (my mother's sister, Mrs. W. J. Bream) lived right next door to your mother, and I was a frequent visitor there.

I do not recall what doctor attended your mother, at your birth. If you will forward the affidavit forms to me, with the following data, viz.—your birthdate; your mother's age when you were born, and when she died; your father, Mr. Edwards's initials; his age when you were born; his age at death—I will make the necessary affidavit, and my brother, Dr. Frank B. Edmundson, of this city, who is slightly older than I am, will contribute to the document.

Best of luck, and hope I can help you out,

Yours, etc.,
T. P. Edmundson
6223 5th Avenue
Pittsburgh, Pennsylvania

"Your mother was my father's niece. . . ." As late as 1942, my grandfather had had cousins living in Pittsburgh, Pennsylvania, and my own father had never heard of them. *Edmundson* . . . another family name.

I went on to the next letter.

Oct. 21st, 1942

Dear Charles,

There appears to be a fly in the ointment. I was born in 1891 and Frank in 1887. Sorry. Will do anything I can, but apparently they mean what they say.

Mean what? I wondered.

So—let me know if I can really help out.

Yours, etc.
T. P. Edmundson

My grandfather had pursued the matter. There were more letters and a legal paper.

Sat. 11/14/42

Sorry, Charles—Just returned from the South to find your letter here. Believe that your best bet would be to have Mother—Mrs. Margaret H. Edmundson—and her sister—Mrs. Sophie C. Bream (6621 Jackson St., Pgh.) do the certification, rather than Frank and I. So, am returning

the other affidavits. Will be glad to have
them do this if you will forward me the
forms. Also if you don't have to have them
in duplicate, don't do so, as this will save
$1.00 in notary fees. . . .

I laughed at that. It sounded like my father,
extravagant in big things, cautious in small.

12/4/42

Dear Charles,

Your papers will reach you in a day or
two. The notary will mail them directly to
you. I will pay her.

Frank told me to tell you that you are
eligible to belong to the Sons of the Am.
Revolution, and that any time you so desire
to write to him at 5317 5th Ave.

Best to you,
T. P. Edmundson

I looked over the previous paper. That name
. . . Margaret Edmundson. I straightened. That
was Aunt Meg's name. And she'd been born a de-
cade before this correspondence. I'd always
thought Edmundson was a Carlisle name. They
both sounded Scottish. Had my grandfather given
Aunt Meg that name because of something told
him by Great-grandmother Faith? It was something to ask my grandmother.

All at once the unknown branch of the family was gathering shape and form.

I opened the legal paper, expecting it to be the returned, unused affidavit. I was wrong.

STATE OF PENNSYLVANIA:

        ss:

COUNTY OF ALLEGHENY:

MARGARET H. EDMUNDSON, being duly sworn, says:

I am 82 years of age and reside at No. 6223 Fifth Avenue, Pittsburgh, Pa.

I know William Charles Edwards and Charles Edward Carlisle to be one and the same person. His mother was my niece. Her maiden name was Faith A. I. Dryden, and she was a citizen of the United States by birth.

Faith A. I. Dryden was married to William Charles Edwards, also, to the best of my knowledge, a citizen of the United States. A son, William Charles Edwards, was born of this marriage in 1897.

In 1903 my niece received—

I drew my breath in sharply.

In 1903 my niece received a decree in divorce from William Charles Edwards.

In 1906 my niece married Douglas Scott Carlisle at Trinity Evangelical and Reformed Church in Wilkinsburg, Pennsylvania, and I was a witness of this wedding.

In 1908 Mr. and Mrs. Douglas Scott Carlisle and her son, William Charles Edwards, moved to New York City, N.Y. From that time on they brought up her son under the name of Charles Edward Carlisle, and to the best of my knowledge and belief he has been known by that name ever since.

Margaret H. Edmundson

Sworn to before me on this *5th* day of *December, 1942*

Faith Dryden Edwards Carlisle had not been a widow. She had been divorced. I had had a great-grandmother who in 1903 had dared to be a divorcée and raise her son alone. Never mind that she had married again, three years later. I knew— how well I knew, from Stephanie and Paulina— that it took courage to contemplate that. And in 1903!

In 1903 my grandfather had been only half the age that John Henry was right now.

I sat there in the old cemetery in the fading afternoon light. The first of the autumn leaves swirled slowly by me, and my thoughts were swirling with them.

I had started on this crusade in the hope of proving I was a Carlisle, because it was Carlisle strength and Carlisle survivalship I had always clung to. Now, like the hope that was supposed to be the last god-gift out of the mythic Pandora's box, I was finding those same qualities becoming personified in the great-grandmother who had become a Carlisle only by her second marriage.

NINE

ON SATURDAY an interested group of us kids, larger than it would have been if the football game hadn't been rained out, gathered in our kitchen. Mother had gone to Clyde's in Georgetown with Paulina for omelets and a heart-to-heart talk, and Dad was out somewhere with Ali. I had a sneaking suspicion that that was just as well. They might not have appreciated the fact that Bruce, Greg, Steff, and Alaiyo, not to mention Asagai, were happily going through the family papers along with Suzi, Tracy, John Henry, and myself. And Scott, who was at the kitchen counter making a pot of minestrone large enough to feed an army and occasionally reading over someone's shoulder.

"Okay," I said briskly, "where do we go from here?"

The contents of the inlaid box and of Gadge's mailing folder were spread from one end of the table to the other. Also on the table were two family photo albums; pictures from both Mom and Dad's and Grandfather and Gadge's weddings; Douglas Scott Carlisle's gold pocket watch, which would be Scott's someday; and a bunch of other family objects. One thing had led to another, as it usually does when people start reminiscing. Asagai was fascinated.

"I had no idea Americans valued the spirits of their ancestors," he murmured, studying a miniature that Aunt Faith had painted of a Revolutionary War grave marker that stood on the grounds of Carlisle's Hope. "What is this, please, that your kinsman writes of? Sons of Am. Revolution?"

"Sons of the American Revolution," Scott supplied. "Hey, Jess, that might be a place to contact."

I made a note. "What else have we got?" I asked.

John Henry looked up from his careful list. "Four letters from T. P. Edmundson. *Dr.* T. P. Edmundson, the return address says. His brother and his father were doctors too. The affidavit from his mother, Margaret, the affidavit from Grandfather on how he was born William Charles Edwards and took the name of Carlisle, the letter from the church about his baptism, and a draft of a letter to the Pittsburgh Board of Education asking whether school records there show his birth date, since Grandfather had to apply for a delayed birth certificate."

"Is the birth certificate here?"

"Nope. But there's a scorched notice that says something about an attached certified copy being an exact copy of his birth record." John Henry studied the burn marks with interest. "Maybe this is a clue. Maybe a lot of records got burned up in a fire."

"And maybe Gadge started to throw this stuff out with the trash sometime and then pulled it back," Suzi said, deflating him. "Anyway, the certificate's not here." She poked through the papers. "Grandfather must have written the New York Board of Education too. Here's a letter from a public school in the Bronx saying that their records show 'Charles Carlisle, father's name Douglas, born December 2, 1898.' Hey, that's a year later than what the Edmundsons said!"

I was beginning to realize that genealogical research was not easy. Eagleton was going to get his pound of flesh out of me.

We went on with John Henry's list. There was a carbon of Grandfather's letter to the Bureau of Vital Statistics in the City-County Building in Pittsburgh, asking for a certified copy of the record of his mother's second marriage. There was a similar carbon, this time to the Clerk of the Court, asking for a "photostatic copy of the original complaint and the judgment rendered in the divorce proceedings between Faith Dryden Edwards and William Edwards, probably sometime between December 2, 1898 and April 25, 1906."

And then there were the replies Grandfather had received:

> Faith Dryden Edwards by her next friend Jas. N. Dryden vs. William Charles Edwards, April Term, 1903. In divorce.

> Nov. 9, 1903 Decree granted, Respondent to pay record. If you desire certified copy of said Decree in Divorce, upon receipt of certified check . . .

> Testimony in divorce shows one son born of this marriage on Dec. 2, 1897. Name or birthplace of this child is not indicated.

> However, records of City of Pittsburgh, Bureau of Vital Statistics, show record of birth of William Charles Edwards . .

> . . do not show that you were adopted or how you acquired your present name. Perhaps this took place in some other county or state.

We were all disgusted by that question about color, although Asagai was rather pleased at hav-

MEMORANDUM OF MARRIAGE LICENSE RECORD
IN THE ORPHANS' COURT OF ALLEGHENY COUNTY

Name of bridegroom __Douglas Scott Carlisle__   Age __30__

Date of Birth __May 8, 1975__

Occupation _____

Residence __611 Coal St. Pgh. Pa.__   Prior marriage __none__

Color _____ Place of Birth __Maryland__

If prior marriage, how and when dissolved _____

Name of person consenting when a minor _____

Name of bride __Faith Dryden Edwards__   Age __30__

Date of Birth __July 2, 1875__

Occupation _____

Residence __611 Coal St. Pgh. Pa.__   Prior marriage __once__

Color _____ Place of Birth __Virginia__

If prior marrige, how and when dissolved __divorce__

Name of person consenting when a minor _____

Date of issue of license __April 25, 1906__

Performed at __Wilkinsburg, Pa.__

Date of ceremony __April 25, 1906__

Ceremony performed by __Lewis Robb__

ing what he'd heard about America's race history confirmed. "You notice the clerk didn't even bother filling out that part of the form," I pointed out.

"I notice a couple of other things left out," Scott commented. "Like occupation. What did Douglas Scott Carlisle do for a living? I don't think we ever heard."

Stephanie looked startled. "I thought he lived on that fabulous estate you always talk about. Carlisle's Hope."

Involuntarily I winced and looked at John Henry. But Stone Face just said matter-of-factly, "Carlisle's Hope isn't an estate. It's a family farm. There used to be lots of them around there. And Douglas Scott Carlisle didn't own it in 1906. His grandfather did." He turned to Asagai. "If you're interested in what Americans value, maybe you'd like to see my coin collection. Some came from the Carlisle's Hope attic, and some my dad gave me. I'll go get them."

He made for the door. "Let him go," Scott said. "The kid wants to collect himself in private."

"I didn't know he knew so much about Carlisle history," I said soberly.

"Probably Aunt Faith's influence. He's been living at Carlisle's Hope, remember."

"Who is this Aunt Faith of Carlisle's Hope? If I am not intruding," Asagai asked politely.

Tracy, Suzi, Scott, and I took turns explaining.

As we did I could feel something easing—in the atmosphere of the room, and in myself. We had needed to talk about Aunt Faith more than we knew. I felt Greg's eyes on me and smiled at him.

John Henry came back with his coin folders, and Asagai was impressed. So was Greg. "Some of these are pretty rare."

"Can they be purchased anywhere?" asked Asagai. "What do you call them—*script,* and *half dismes*? I would like to take a collection like this back to my brother. He, too, collects."

"There's a coin dealer in Old Town, and there are some in D.C., too, who would know where to look. People can still buy them—if they can come up with enough money," Greg added.

Alaiyo winked at me. Asagai was the eldest son of a tribal chieftain, and money was not a problem for him.

Suzi was more interested in the possibilities opened up by the documents than in old coins. "Six eleven Coal Street. The marriage license says they were both living at 611 Coal Street. Do you think—"

"I think that was the address where they were going to be living once they were married." Tracy gave her a look. "That was 1906, remember. Don't get liberated ideas."

I had gone back to the matter of occupations. "I wonder what Great-grandmother Faith did?

·And don't tell me that was 1906! She had to have done *something*. She had a child to support."

"Alimony," Stephanie suggested from long experience.

"Did they have it in 1906? I didn't even know divorce was legal then. What do you suppose the grounds were? They must have had to be really serious."

"What were your great-grandmother's grounds for divorce?" Greg asked practically.

We searched the papers. Nowhere were they stated, not even in the copy of the certificate Grandfather had gotten from the Prothonotary.

"Eagleton won't like that," Alaiyo pointed out. "He expects all *i*'s dotted and all *t*'s crossed."

"Tough. It's *my* family, not his!"

"It's also your research-project grade."

"So I'll find the missing pieces. I never said I was expecting an easy A," I snapped.

By the time Scott's soup was done, we had a list of what to do next:

1. Look in Pittsburgh phone book for any Edmundsons, Edwards, or Drydens.
2. Write the Office of the Prothonotary and ask for a transcript of the divorce testimony.
3. Write the Pittsburgh newspaper. (Newspapers seemed to love stories of the reunions of long-lost relatives.)

"The relatives in those letters can't still be alive," Suzi objected. "They were lots older than Grandfather, and he'd be around ninety now."

"So maybe *they* have grandchildren. Maybe we have a lot of cousins we don't know about," I answered. The thought was fascinating.

I went on with the list:

4. Write the church where Grandfather was baptized and Great-grandmother Faith and Douglas Scott Carlisle were married.
5. Try the Sons of the American Revolution.

It was at this point that we heard the front door open. I scooped up all the papers and stuffed them inside my notebook. Mother and Paulina came into the kitchen, loaded down with bundles.

"We've been buying out Georgetown," Mother announced. "What have you been up to?"

I started to say Looking at John Henry's coins, which was not quite a lie, but Mother looked at the stove and found her own answer to the question.

"Oh, Scott! I hope you didn't use all the groceries I bought this morning! We're having dinner guests tomorrow night."

From the way Paulina was preening, I gathered she and Ali were among those invited. "We'll get out of the kitchen so you can check the refrigerator while Scott cleans up," I said quickly. Clutching the notebook and the box, I left the kitchen. Suzi and John Henry had already skinned out. The others followed.

When I came downstairs after hiding the evidence, Greg was still in the front hall.

"Do I get the feeling your mother's not keen on your research project?"

"*I* get that feeling. Don't ask me the reasons. Anyway, they're my great-grandparents, and I have a right to know the facts about them."

I didn't get any further on my research that weekend, because Greg and I went bowling that night. On Sunday, leaving the house to Mother and her dinner party seemed like a good idea, so all us kids ended up eating at the Barillos'. Bruce and Greg cooked, because Caroline was at my parents' party. Afterward we watched movies on their VCR. It was a nice, lazy evening.

It wasn't till late Sunday night, as I was getting my stuff together for school the next morning, that I thought about the Carlisle mystery again.

And now it was my great-grand*mother* whom I had a passionate need to know. Not just the bare facts of the papers, or her likeness in the photograph, or her Star of Bethlehem quilt, but her *self*. Had she been like Aunt Faith? Had she been like me? How had she reacted to the breakup of her world? And how had she survived?

TEN

IT DID not take long on Monday for my excitement about the project to vanish. Eagleton waltzed into English class and reminded us that this was the thirtieth of September and the due date for our research projects was exactly two weeks away.

"Your thesis statements are due next Monday," he said with a thin smile. The sadist, I thought; he was enjoying our suffering. "By that I mean a one- or two-sentence paragraph on the assumption you hope to prove. I'm sure I need not remind you that it must be objective. The rest of your paper will present the proof, or disproof, as the case may be, backed up by solid data. Subjective conclusions will not be accepted."

There went what I was really researching—the strength of Faith Carlisle's character and her peace of mind.

"You could write about the legal question of the Carlisle name," Greg suggested later. "What made your grandfather a Carlisle, as the FBI was apparently satisfied he was? Legal rulings should be great for Eagleton."

"What interests me is what made Grandfather a Carlisle on the *inside*," I said darkly. "I don't have time to go plowing into lawbooks! And another thing. Two weeks isn't going to be time enough to get answers to those research letters. I haven't even started writing them yet!"

Greg gave me a quizzical look. "I've got news for you. The telephone's been invented."

I turned red. I should explain that while I spend hours on the telephone with Steff and Alaiyo, I am the world's worst chicken when it comes to making calls to people I don't know.

"Want me to call the courthouse about the divorce transcript?" Greg offered.

"No." I didn't want Greg to think I was a coward, and the courthouse probably wouldn't give out information to a non family member anyway.

Mother had to make calls like this all the time when she was doing journalistic research. I'd heard her often. I'd heard about—and overheard—calls Dad had placed around the world, dealing with foreign telephone systems and antagonistic foreign diplomats. So I'd phone the Pittsburgh courthouse myself.

Our spell of late summer had been broken that day by soggy rain. After I slogged home and dried myself off, I took over the family room and its telephone. Mother was tapping away upstairs on her word processor, which meant she was immersed and had the extension up there unplugged. So she couldn't pick up the receiver and accidentally hear what I was doing.

For a minute temptation beckoned me: I could pretend I was Mother calling for *The Washington Post*. But I rejected that idea because I knew she would have killed me. I did, however, borrow Suzi's version of Paulina's throaty voice. Anything so the people at the Pittsburgh courthouse wouldn't think I was just some nosy kid!

I'd stopped at the Alexandria library on the way home to get phone numbers, so I reached the courthouse easily, using Dad's long-distance calling number. I reached the Office of the Prothonotary, who turned out to be Chief Clerk of the Court. I reached a nice lady named Mrs. Saunders, who was fascinated to learn that Miss Jessamyn Carlisle was researching Pittsburgh family history for possible publication. (Okay, so I fibbed a little.)

"Of course, you can read what's in the transcript if it still exists. We have kept records going back further than 1903, but some were damaged. There's no way of knowing whether this divorce transcript was among them. Do you know the approximate date?"

"I have the exact date and the case number." I supplied them.

"That will make things much easier, but it can't be checked right now. We'll have to send someone over to McKeesport, where the old records are kept. We'll call you back next week."

"Don't call us. We'll call you," I said hastily. We set it up that I'd call a week from that afternoon.

I was left feeling antsy. I was psyched for action, but what next?

Write the Pittsburgh paper? I had that address and phone number too.

Suzi came in and, finding me struggling, said, "Oh, for Pete's sake, phone 'em!" and then placed the call herself. I listened as she was transferred from person to person and then hung up, scowling.

"That pain in the you-know-what on the switchboard wouldn't put me through to the feature editor! She just switched me to the archives, and they couldn't do anything if I didn't 'provide dates on which the relevant articles appeared'!" She mimicked the patronizing tone.

"Give me the phone," I said grimly, and rooted through the old papers.

The church where Faith and Douglas Scott Carlisle were married still had the same phone number as when Grandfather had written them. It also had a lovely secretary.

"How interesting! I've been doing some genealogical research too. Hold the phone and I'll look up your great-grandparents' records."

There was a long pause during which I crossed all my fingers and toes.

"Here it is," she said at last. "Your grandfather was baptized William Charles Edwards on November 12, 1899. Reverend Alspach didn't fill in any birth dates nor the names of the parents, but I looked a bit earlier and found that Faith Dryden Edwards and William Charles Edwards joined the church that same month. Their address is given as 611 Coal Street."

That was the same address that was on the Carlisle marriage license.

"What do you have on her remarriage?" I gave the dates.

"We don't have any record of that at all."

"The marriage license says she and Mr. Carlisle were married by the Reverend Lewis Robb of Trinity Church on April 25, 1906."

The woman's voice quickened. "That's very interesting. Mr. Robb became pastor in 1905. Perhaps the ceremony wasn't in the sanctuary. Although it still should have been entered in our records."

"Maybe she waited till a new minister came because the old one wouldn't perform a marriage for a divorcée!" Suzi suggested immediately, as I hung up.

"Maybe the minister didn't enter it because the church board would not have approved. We don't know. And it doesn't look as if we're going to find out. So don't go putting two and two together and getting twenty-five!"

"Until you get your stuffy hard evidence, I have as much right to fantasize about my great-grandmother as you do," Suzi informed me haughtily.

I reported the results of this telephoning to my research aides the next afternoon. Everyone who had been present in our kitchen on Saturday was there. Asagai produced a beautifully lettered genealogical chart of my family.

"I'm interested in genealogical lines. My people kept them as oral history for centuries." He shrugged off my astonished gratitude. The chart, in exquisite calligraphy, was far more than just a generational listing. Asagai added the latest information. Then I fastened the chart to the bulletin board and we studied it.

"It's a lot easier to see how everybody fits in this way," John Henry said, impressed.

"It's a lot easier to see all the missing links," I added. The passage of time was weighing on my mind.

EDMUNDSON-DRYDEN-CHAMBERS-CARLISLE GENEALOGY

James Dryden *m.* Pamela R. Edmundson W. F. Edmundson *m.* Margaret H. Sophie *m.* W. J. Bream

Clarence Dryden   Faith A. I. Dryden

Frank B.   T. F. Edmundson
Edmundson

m. (1) William Charles Edwards
(divorced)

m. (2) Douglas Scott Carlisle

William Charles Edward Carlisle   Douglas Edward Carlisle   Charles Scott Carlisle   Faith Dryden Carlisle
m. Katherine Allison Sterling   *m.* Jenetta S. Vandever   (killed in Vietnam)   *m.* Henry Squier

Margaret Edmundson Carlisle   Tracy Louise   Scott Thomas   Jessamyn Faith   Susan Clare   John Henry Squier
m. Samuel Pierce

Carol Pierce
m. Peter Craig

"You know your thesis statement about the legal grounds for having a right to the Carlisle name?" Alaiyo put in. "Don't forget my dad's a lawyer."

I hadn't thought of that. I nodded gratefully.

"The university has a law library. I could look stuff up, if I knew what I was looking for," Bruce offered. He slid his arm around Tracy's waist. "Maybe your sister could help me."

"Maybe I could find a foxy law student to look it up for me," Tracy replied with a smirk.

Bruce said, "Oh, yeah?" and pulled her closer, and I told them to cut it out, this was serious.

"The thesis is due in six days, and the finished paper is due the Monday after. Twenty pages minimum." I looked at Steff and Alaiyo. "How much have you done on yours?"

"I'm doing mine on the Ashanti kingdoms," Alaiyo said innocently, and I grinned. Eagleton couldn't know that Alaiyo did a lot of digging into that last year, and now was just supplementing it with what you might call hands-on research with Asagai.

"I may not even be here that Monday," Stephanie said tersely, her chin trembling.

"What's happened?" I asked quickly.

"Not now."

Alaiyo looked from me to Steff. "Is it your fath—"

"I said, *not now*." Stephanie turned her back.

In the awkward silence that followed, Greg cleared his throat and handed me a notebook. "I made a couple of phone calls yesterday too. I called the Carnegie Library in Pittsburgh. Scott told me it was good for research."

"Hit pay dirt?" Scott asked with interest, and Greg nodded.

"A lady in the Pennsylvania History division was very helpful. She said to send her specific questions and she'll see what she can find. She's going to try to check whether there are any Edmundson, Edwards, or Dryden descendants still in Pittsburgh. And she gave me the phone number of the Historical Society."

Greg spread his papers out on the table and we all gathered around, intent. "See? The Homewood district is a section of Pittsburgh now. So is Wilkinsburg." He pointed them out on a map; where he'd gotten it from I did not know. "This is where Bennett Street is, where your grandfather was born. And this is where Coal Street is. The woman said there were only three buildings, frame houses, on the street at the turn of the century. But there are no street numbers on the city map she has, so she can't tell exactly where 611 stood. And," Greg finished triumphantly, "the church where your great-grandparents were married is on Coal Street also, and since the church secretary said that was the original church building, the house where Faith Carlisle lived with both her husbands must have been only a couple of doors from the church!"

"Greg Barillo, I love you," I said fervently. And, of course, turned red.

Suzi shared her speculations about the living situation of Great-grandmother and her second husband before they were married and was thoroughly hooted down.

Tracy looked thoughtful. "Maybe she took in boarders. After her divorce, I mean. That was a respectable way for a married woman to make money in those days."

Nineteen-oh-three. Faith Edwards had been twenty-eight then, and her son had been six. I thought about that; I thought about Gadge being widowed with a toddler; I thought about Paulina and Stephanie.

"Hey, I have to get home or my mother will fry me," Alaiyo exclaimed. "She has a late meeting at her office and I promised I'd start dinner." That got the others moving also. Bruce gave everybody rides. I cleared the table, finishing just as Mother came downstairs.

"What have you all been up to?" she inquired, tying on an apron. "I heard Bruce leaving, and John Henry looks happy; I met him on the stairs."

"Working on term papers. Alaiyo's doing hers on the Ashantis."

"How convenient." Mother laughed. She rummaged through the refrigerator, brought out the remainder of Scott's minestrone and some frozen chicken, and tossed me a head of lettuce. "Here, shred this," she said, heading for the microwave. Then she saw the bulletin board and stopped.

"Jessamyn, what is this?" she asked in a peculiar voice.

I had forgotten to put away the genealogy chart.

"Oh, that," I said airily. "Asagai made that up for me. Isn't it neat?" She could take the word *neat* in any sense she wanted. "He got the names from those letters of Grandfather's and—"

"Jessamyn Faith Carlisle, have you dragged everybody and his brother in on this so-called research for Mr. Eagleton?"

Whenever my mother calls me Jessamyn Faith, I shiver.

"I wouldn't say *drag*. They're real interested."

"I'll bet," Mother said grimly. "And I'll bet it's going home to Caroline and Paulina, and from Paulina to Ali, and have you considered where else?"

I stared at her. "*Mother!* In the first place Caroline and Paulina are friends of yours. And in the second place so what if they did say something?"

"In the first place," Mother said distinctly, "I trust Caroline implicitly, but if her sons come home chatting about interesting tidbits they pick up here in general conversation, she has a perfect right to assume they're public knowledge. In the second place I don't trust Paulina farther than she can see without her glasses. In the third place—"

"In the third place," I interrupted, "what difference does it make? It's not as if we had any skeletons to dig out of closets. What are you afraid of?"

Then I got a different kind of shiver. I looked Mother straight in the eyes, and I sat down.

"That's it exactly," Mother said quietly. "We don't know whether there are any skeletons or not." She sat down too.

"What difference does it make?" I repeated shakily. "If you're thinking about . . . insanity, or adultery, or murder, or wife-beating. . . ." I dragged out the specters that could have been grounds for divorce a hundred years ago. "Those people are all dead and gone now. It doesn't matter. We're *us*. The Carlisles." I was repeating what Dad had told me, almost like a litany.

"We're us," Mother said. "With diplomatic passports. Your father has security clearance. He has four years till he can retire from the U.S.I.A. with full pension, and then he may want to go into politics. Can you honestly be sure that whatever you might dig up about his bloodlines couldn't hurt his chances?"

She went to the microwave, leaving me stunned. But not too stunned to wrestle with my conscience.

Could I honestly say that my need to know superseded any risks? Had I really been "braving the unknown," or had my research been another manifestation of the flounder syndrome—the need to feel safe, to cling doggedly to roots?

One thing was sure. I'd opened a Pandora's box, and it was too late to slam the lid down now.

ELEVEN

I PUT the What Became of William Charles Edwards mystery on the back burner after that, but not because I was afraid of what I might find out. I thought of the worst possibilities that could exist, and none of them really affected me at all. I didn't feel connected with William Edwards. Quite honestly, finding I had the blood of a mass murderer in my veins couldn't bother me as much as had finding out I did *not* have Carlisle blood.

Actually I could see Mother's point about Dad's career. I'd been a Foreign Service brat long enough to know about rumor mills and political smears. So that was one reason for the back burner.

Another was that there wasn't much I could do anyway until I heard from the Office of the Prothonotary next Monday. And another was that other people and their family troubles were suddenly more important.

Alaiyo and I were really alarmed about Stephanie. Always fragile, she began to look as if she were made of tissue paper, and there were purple shadows underneath her eyes. On Wednesday afternoon Paulina's lawyer told her in no uncertain terms that she would be in big trouble if she refused to allow Steff's father to have visitation rights. For the first time since the grand romance with Ali started, Paulina was popping pills and washing them down with booze. I knew about this the same way I knew about the grand romance— from my mother, who was on the receiving end of Paulina's hysteria.

Steff came to school Thursday looking like a walking skeleton. Alaiyo and I held a worried consultation in the girls' room.

"Butt in?" asked Alaiyo.

"We have to," I said boldly. "What do the counselors call it? A crisis intervention. *Somebody'd* better intervene before she turns into a basket case like her mother."

"Okay," Alaiyo said somberly, "let's get her

over to my house this afternoon. Kidnap her, if necessary. My parents will be at their offices, so we'll have privacy."

Up in Alaiyo's room, with its exotic mix of Chippendale antiques and African carvings, we confronted Stephanie. And Steff, in a voice like cracked glass, said she didn't know what we were talking about.

"We're talking about dealing with reality, girl," Alaiyo said with brutal tenderness. "You can't keep on trying to live in a fantasy."

Stephanie's eyes flared. "*I'm* not the one living in a fantasy—"

"The fantasy that your natural father doesn't exist?" Alaiyo countered. "The fantasy that you can escape what's happening? The fantasy that you can avoid feeling anything?"

"Not letting your emotions out at all can be just as bad as being too emotional," I said gently.

It struck me that that was an odd thing to be saying to Stephanie. I've always thought she over-dramatized her feelings. It dawned on me now that that was what it had always been—dramatization, *talk*, but never real emotion that was allowed to escape in tears or anger and be gone.

Quite suddenly Stephanie broke. She sobbed and sobbed, great wrenching spasms that left her spent and shaking, and she wouldn't let us touch her. I ached to hold her close and comfort her. But that was a fantasy too, I realized—the notion that we could put our arms around someone and keep her safe.

"What are you afraid of?" Alaiyo asked quietly.

"I'm not afraid!"

"Oh, yes, you are," I said. "You're right where I was the night I found out about not being a Carlisle: standing in quicksand."

"It's quicksand, all right," Stephanie said grimly, sitting up on the bed and flinging back her damp hair. She stared at her hands, at the thin fingers that kept lacing and unlacing. "I don't know how much more I can take," she said simply. "Not just never knowing what my last name is or whom I'm supposed to call my father. I don't know how much longer I can be my mother's keeper. *She's* the one who's supposed to be the parent."

She looked at me. "Your parents groan about who Suzi's friends are, and what she may be smoking or may be doing. It drives Suzi crazy, but they're the parents, and they're acting like parents."

"And Suzi," I said ruefully, "is acting like a five-year-old. Or a thirty-five-year-old, depending on your point of view."

"My mother," Stephanie said carefully, "is well over forty, and I have to be *her* parent. Without any of the authority your parents have over

Suzi. Without any rights. Not even the right to divorce a parent who deserted me."

"Being a minor is hell," Alaiyo agreed. "All kids know that. And then forget it the minute they turn into parents themselves. But that's *reality*, Steff. You have to accept what you can't change, and concentrate on changing what you can."

"Thank you. I already know about Alcoholics Anonymous," Stephanie said coldly.

"Then why don't you try it sometime?" I asked.

"You think I haven't? I can't change my mother, and I know it. I also know I can't get away from her, not till I'm eighteen. And even then she'll still have . . . strings in my blood vessels." Stephanie's metaphors were decidedly mixed, but neither Alaiyo nor I felt like laughing. Stephanie took a deep breath.

"I can understand why my mother's popping pills. I really can. They're all over our house, and sometimes I think, it would just be so easy. . . ."

Over her head Alaiyo's eyes met mine in alarm.

Abruptly Stephanie jumped up, the brittle mask in place again. "I have to get home. I'm going to call a cab, Jess. You want to share it?"

"I'll call my mom to get both of us," I offered, but Steff shook her head. I suspected she didn't want anyone else to see her in this state. Since I couldn't let her go home alone, I shared her cab, saw her into her house, where fortunately Paulina was home and sober, then directed the taxi driver to the Flounder House.

My family was already around the dinner table. Dad took a look at me, and any reproof about tardiness died on his lips. Afterward I got both my parents off alone and related my afternoon. They looked sober.

"I could kill Paulina," Mother said somberly. "I really could. Stephanie's right. She could handle her other problems if Paulina would just get herself together."

"If Paulina got herself together," Dad pointed out, "Stephanie wouldn't *have* the other problems."

"But the problems are there. Even if things change, it might not be soon enough." I told them Stephanie's comment about the attraction of her mother's pills.

"I was planning to work all day tomorrow," Mother said grimly. "I'll have Paulina over for lunch instead."

I kept Stephanie's mind off her troubles the next afternoon by getting her to come with me to the library, where we both did research for our papers. Afterward we bumped into Scott and Greg, who had been showing John Henry the store that sold old coins. Then we all stopped in at a fast-food place and had burgers and large milk shakes.

Both Steff and John Henry started looking better. A faint trace of color even came into Stephanie's face, and she looked quite pretty. It occurred to me, not for the first time, that if Scott would finally discover girls, he'd be awfully good for Stephanie.

We reached home to find Mother cooking up a storm. "And there's a letter from Japan for John Henry," she said brightly. John Henry ran for it.

I looked at Mother, and she shook her head slightly. Clearly this was not the time to ask about her lunch with Paulina.

It wasn't the time to say much to John Henry either. Uncle Henry had tried his best, but his letter was still pretty skimpy. It listed the places in Japan where he had to go on business, but it didn't say anything about taking John Henry with him. It said stuff like he knew John Henry would be a brave young man and do his best to obey his uncle Doug and aunt Jenetta, and try not to be a nuisance or make work for us. It said he was sending John Henry some old Japanese coins and a samurai sword, but it didn't say a word about when Uncle Henry would be coming home.

John Henry read it aloud at the dinner table and then said he wasn't very hungry, thank you, so could he please be excused because he felt like going for a walk.

"Let him go by himself," Dad said when Scott half rose to follow him.

Mother sighed. "Poor kid. It's finally registered on him that he's become an add-on here."

Stephanie was right. Being a minor, not having any autonomy, could be hell.

On Saturday a box for John Henry arrived at the airport Customs office. It contained the samurai sword and other good things. Scott offered to help John Henry hang the sword on his bedroom wall; Mother suggested John Henry might like to do some redecorating in the attic bedroom; and Dad even offered grandly to buy a small TV for his room. John Henry was perfectly polite about all the suggestions, but totally uninterested. I could have cried.

"He's still in shock," Greg told me later.

"If it was anybody but John Henry, I'd think he was stoned."

"That's how shock affects some people," Greg said. "I remember." And he asked John Henry, just John Henry, over to the Barillo house for Sunday night supper and a lengthy examination of his late father's stamp collection.

Sunday was a gorgeous day, so gorgeous that the family scattered in all directions to enjoy it. Mother and I had tea in the back garden and brought each other up to date regarding John Henry, Stephanie, and Paulina.

"If it's any comfort to Stephanie," Mother told me, "Paulina's moving heaven and earth to keep Stephanie's father from her. She probably won't win, and I think she's making a big mistake.

One of these days Steff should see her father—for her own sake, not for his. But she doesn't have to worry that Paulina will give in easily."

"She's more worried that Paulina will do something desperate, or that she'll sell out in exchange for more child-support payments," I said flatly.

Mother looked shocked.

"I can't help it," I said. "That's the way Stephanie feels."

I looked at my mother sitting quietly in the old redwood chair. I looked around our back garden, with its grape arbor and herb garden and walls of faded brick, and an impulse surged through me like a tidal wave. An impulse to count my blessings. Because it didn't really matter whose blood ran in my veins. I, too, had "strings in my blood vessels," as Stephanie had said, and to my eternal good fortune, *my* strings were a blessing. If blood was thicker than water, love was thicker than blood; it could reach out to those who were kin or kin in spirit only—like John Henry; like Stephanie. It could even create kinship—like the kinship between Douglas Scott Carlisle and my grandfather.

And feeling that kind of kinship with persons who actually were my own flesh and blood was, as Aunt Faith would have put it, a gift of grace.

TWELVE

No KIDDING, I actually forgot that Monday was the day I was supposed to phone back the Office of the Prothonotary. By then the question of the Edwardses' divorce grounds scarcely seemed important.

For one thing Eagleton wasted ten minutes of class time reminding us that our research paper deadline was one week off, which meant that I'd better come up with a thesis statement very fast. It was due that day, of course, a little matter that had also escaped my mind. I told Eagleton a whopper of a fib about what had happened to my homework, and fled to Alaiyo in panic.

"Come home with me tomorrow afternoon and talk to Dad," she volunteered. "I know he's all tied up today, but he'll have time tomorrow." Her eyes flicked to Stephanie. "Why don't both you guys come?" she said casually.

Alaiyo was still very worried about Stephanie, and so was I. I was worried about John Henry too. I made a note to tell Dad that the next time he was on the phone with Uncle Henry, he might give my uncle some pointers about how to be a successful parent.

When I got back to Old Town after school, I walked through the misty rain around to the coin store and bought John Henry a coin for his collection. Gifts couldn't make up for the absence of his father, but they could at least show that I cared. I only wished I could do something concrete to help Stephanie. What she needed was a lawyer and a therapist, and both of those were too expensive for my budget.

I went home to find Mother reading the phone bill, and not looking pleased.

"Jess, really! Do you know what this 'fishing expedition' of yours is costing?" I opened my mouth and she cut me off. "Don't bother asking how I knew it was you. Who else would be making calls to Pittsburgh?"

"I'll pay for them," I said hastily. "And they haven't all been made on our phone bill. Greg did some calling for me."

"Do you mean to tell me you have all your friends prying into our family secrets also? Jess, I told you—"

"Don't start!" I shouted rudely, and made for the stairs. Featherstone followed. We took refuge in my room. I slammed the door, which was childish but made me feel better.

A few minutes later the door handle turned. "I'm not going to discuss it!" I said sharply.

"Don't take my head off," Suzi retorted, coming in. "I just wondered if you'd heard about the divorce testimony yet."

I stared at her blankly, then scrambled for my notebook and the phone.

"Want me to leave?" Suzi asked discreetly.

"Don't be ridiculous. It's your family history too." Actually I was glad to have Suzi, for my heart was pounding.

I reached the Office of the Prothonotary and got the nice lady.

"Oh, yes, Miss Carlisle," she said cheerfully. "We have the information for you." No, she could not send me a transcript; there was some new law about that that I didn't understand. But she could read the testimony to me over the phone.

"Just a minute!" I blurted out. Suzi thrust a ball-point pen into my hand.

I didn't get it down word for word. I couldn't. But the evidence filed with the Court of Common Pleas came down to this:

1. Faith Dryden Edwards and William Charles Edwards lived at four different Pittsburgh addresses. The last was 611 Coal Street.

2. They had one son, William Charles Edwards, Jr.

3. William Charles Edwards, Sr., worked for the railroad, and between 1899 and 1901 he worked at night.

4. On the night of September 2, 1901 he simply vanished off the face of the earth.

5. Faith Dryden Edwards reported his disappearance to the police, but the police never solved the mystery.

6. After September 2, 1901 Faith Dryden Edwards was the sole support of herself and her child. No money was provided by William Charles Edwards, nor was any information on his whereabouts ever found.

7. After the period prescribed by law, Faith Dryden Edwards, through her father, James Dryden, filed for divorce on the grounds of desertion.

8. William Charles Edwards did not contest the suit. He did not appear in court. A decree of divorce was brought in against him, and court costs were levied against him in absentia.

Which, of course, the court never got. My great-grandfather had disappeared into thin air.

I put the phone down slowly and sat there on the Star of Bethlehem quilt, gazing off into space and feeling drained.

"Maybe he was murdered!" Suzi suggested. "Or maybe he owed a lot of gambling debts he couldn't pay."

"Maybe you've been watching too many old westerns on TV. Pittsburgh wasn't Dodge City."

"How do you know?" Suzi countered. "It was a railroad town. And a coal and steel town." I hadn't known she'd learned so much U.S. history. "Maybe he stole from the railroad and had to run. And the railroad never reported the crime to the police because something crooked had been going on."

"Maybe it doesn't matter," I said quietly.

It really didn't; not anymore. And not, apparently, to my grandfather. His father William Charles Edwards had gone; his father Douglas Scott Carlisle had come. That must have been enough for the deserted boy of not quite four. That, and a mother who had been a Rock of Gibraltar all by herself, like her granddaughter namesake, my Aunt Faith.

So help me God, I found myself thinking that if John Henry had had to lose a parent, it should have been his father, not his mother. It was not a particularly nice thought, but there it was.

"No wonder Grandfather latched on to Douglas Carlisle," I said at last. "He must have recognized the Carlisle heritage as another form of the values he was getting from his mother."

"No wonder," Suzi said practically, "he was so eager to junk his father's name. Old William wasn't much of a role model!"

"We'll never know." But he must have had something, I thought, for Faith Dryden to have married him. Married at twenty-one, mother at twenty-two, deserted at twenty-six; boardinghouse-keeper, trained nurse, divorcée, and then again a wife. What was it Dad always said? "When the going gets tough, the tough get going."

I felt a deep gratitude, which I saw mirrored in my sister's eyes, that we had Edmundson-Dryden and Carlisle strength of character as our birthright. And the Sterlings' too; that was Gadge's family. And Mother's Jersey Dutch Vandever heritage.

By a kind of unspoken agreement neither Suzi nor I said anything about the telephone call at dinner. I told Dad about it privately afterward, and *he* told the rest of the family later that same evening over hot chocolate and marshmallows around the fireplace. Mother couldn't get mad at *him* for bringing it up, since it was his own father's story.

Dad worked in some stuff about how proud he knew his father had been of Faith Carlisle, and how lucky all of us—especially John Henry, he managed to imply—were to have Carlisle's Hope, and parents who loved us, even if they were not always there. So it became a regular *Up the Car-*

lisles session. By the end of it John Henry did look a little better.

On Tuesday I relayed the news to my research cohorts over lunch. Everyone found the story fascinating, and I congratulated myself on damping down speculation as to what had become of William Charles Edwards.

After school Steff and I went home with Alaiyo. We had tea and discussed how mean the Websters were to think Alaiyo was too young to attend a diplomatic reception at Asagai's father's embassy.

Then Mr. and Mrs. Webster came home. "It's not necessary to change your name legally in order to have the legal right to use another name," he told me. "The question hinges on intent to defraud. My daughter, Lee Anne, can call herself Alaiyo till the cows come home; she could even give herself an African last name, which I hope she won't, and sign contracts or be married under it." He chuckled. "It's all right as long as she uses her correct Social Security number and reports all her income to the I.R.S.! But when your grandfather started using the name Carlisle, none of that existed anyway. That's why he could marry as a Carlisle and register his children's births as Carlisles."

"What do you mean, 'intent to defraud'?" I asked.

"Oh, if you took the name of somebody rich or famous, and tried to pass yourself off as that person, or as a relative of that person, you'd be in trouble. Or if you were using a false name to avoid legal responsibilities."

"Like child support," Stephanie said woodenly.

"Exactly. And since Douglas Scott Carlisle didn't legally adopt his stepson, he was under no requirement to support him." Mr. Webster smiled at me. "Apparently none of those problems arose in your grandfather's family."

I thought how lucky Stephanie was that her mother'd never stayed married long enough to maneuver any of the stepfathers into adopting Steff. This way, once the divorces went through, she was free of the race car driver, and the so-called prince, and The Pain.

But not free of her own father, a voice said in my head. Only adoption by someone else could wipe that out.

Stephanie, very pale, said, "What about the child's rights in a divorce? Suppose Mr. Edwards had turned up again. What would have happened?"

"It's not the Edwards case you're really talking about, is it?" Mr. Webster asked gently. "Why don't you and I go into my study so what we say will be covered by the rules of lawyer-client confidentiality? Jess and Alaiyo can go check the kitchen to see if the larder will stretch to include you girls for dinner."

There was chicken, and plenty of it, Mrs. Webster said. But I didn't stay, because when I called home, I got my father and he said to come home right away.

Mrs. Webster drove me. All the way there I was thinking something must have cropped up with Uncle Henry. But it hadn't. I didn't find out a darn thing more until we were sitting around the dinner table and Dad dropped his bomb.

"I thought I should let you know. There's a good chance I'm about to be sent to the Middle East again for a four-year tour of duty."

THIRTEEN

For a stunned moment the kitchen was absolutely still. Then a shaky voice demanded, "What do you mean, they're to send you out again?" The voice was Suzi's. I couldn't say a word.

"Just what I said," Dad repeated. "Overseas relocation."

No more trips back and forth, with Alexandria still home base, but *relocation*. We all knew what that meant. Being uprooted, foreign house, foreign schools, our possessions in storage or sent over by slow freight.

Mother rallied first. "We all knew it could

happen. You're two years short of your quota, aren't you?" Foreign Service officers are supposed to put in a certain number of years overseas before retirement. We'd only been sent home last time because of the crisis in Iran.

Each posting is usually for three or four years. We knew that too.

"It wouldn't be that bad," Scott said thoughtfully. Suzi's eyes were blazing.

"For *you* maybe! You only have one more year of high school and then you'll be off to college. And you're not going out with anybody. What about the rest of us? I'll be darned if I'll spend all four of my high school years overseas, or stuck away in a dormitory! Going to private school as a day student is bad enough!"

"I could finish this year as a boarding student," Tracy said firmly. "Or maybe Caroline would let me stay with her. I want to go to college in D.C. anyway. I could split the cost of Bruce's student apartment then."

"Over my dead body," Mother said emphatically.

John Henry said nothing. I said nothing. I couldn't have spoken to save my soul. It wasn't just that I didn't trust myself to speak; there was no thought I could form in words. Except that I knew, passionately, that I did not want to leave the Flounder House. I didn't want any of us to leave. It was Greg; it was friends; it was Stephanie needing me; it was also much, much more.

Dad put an end to the discussion. "It may not materialize anyway. It's simply in the air, and I thought you should know it." We knew why. More than once in the past our household had been ordered off on immediate notice.

I glanced at my mother. Despite her matter-of-factness she looked shaken. In the five years since we'd come back to Alexandria, Mother had gotten a pretty good part-time career going. She was geared, I knew, to swing it into full-time once Suzi was in senior high. What would happen to it now?

"Another thing." Dad was talking to Mother now, not the rest of us. "Ali's been telling me about a couple of excellent openings in the private sector for Middle East experts with fluent Arabic."

I breathed again.

"Leaving U.S.I.A. early would mean giving up your pension," Mother said slowly.

"It might be worth considering, if the salary figures they bat around the ball park are as high as I've heard."

I could feel myself beginning to get a splitting headache. Suzi looked mutinous; Tracy, troubled; Scott, as though he were weighing options. It wasn't fair, I thought, my eyes stinging. People couldn't survive constant cutting off from their roots.

"We'll discuss this later," Mother said, "when we know more. Right now the pot roast is getting cold."

It could have been frozen solid or made of Styrofoam, for all I cared.

In school the next day I didn't say anything about the possible transfer. I was heading for the bus after school when Stephanie buttonholed me. "Take the late bus, will you? I have to talk to you. Without Alaiyo."

I followed her to our favorite secluded corner of the school library. "What's up?" I demanded. "What did Mr. Webster tell you yesterday?"

"Nothing that's any good! *Parents* have rights in a custody dispute, but not children," Stephanie said bitterly. "*Children* have the right to have the *court* make decisions 'in their best interest,' whether it's what the children want or not. My father's gotten a judge to decide he has a right to see me, and my mother's been served papers to have me ready to be picked up on Friday afternoon. If she doesn't, she'll face kidnapping charges. Mr. Webster says there isn't a thing that we can do."

I made an involuntary sound. Stephanie turned to face me, her eyes absolutely dry. "I won't buy that garbage," she said, except she didn't say garbage, she said a word I'd never expected to hear from Stephanie's lips. "Only I need help. It has to be from you. I can't involve Alaiyo on account of her father."

"What?" I asked guardedly.

"I want to stay over at your house tomorrow night. We'll tell our mothers it's because I'm going away. Friday morning after we leave your house, I won't get on the school bus. I'll go to the airport. I'm going to go somewhere my father won't be able to find me. I'll call my mother to let her know I'm safe," Stephanie added hastily, seeing my face. "I'm going to go to a place and to people she approves of till all this dies down, and I'll make sure she can guess where it is. But she won't *know,* so she can't be charged with hiding me when my father can't find me."

"Steff, it isn't right."

"You think my mother wants me with my father any more than I do?" Stephanie said, eyes flashing. "You think she wouldn't hide me herself, if the penalty weren't so high? She may try yet. I'm just doing it for her so she can't be blamed."

I knew I should say no. I knew all the reasons I should convince Steff she ought to go along with the court order. Maybe I would have done it if I didn't have such gut-wrenching knowledge of what it was like to be uprooted against your will.

I said Steff could stay over with me Thursday night. I did not tell my parents why.

I spent the remainder of the afternoon in my bedroom, working on the research paper, hammering Faith Carlisle's story into the dry form Eagleton would accept. When I went down to dinner, nobody was talking about last night's bombshell, and Mother was wondering where John Henry had gone to.

"He said he was going to the coin store," Scott reported. "Greg and I saw him on King Street after school." Fortunately John Henry walked in at that moment and apologized for being late. The dinner-table conversation was devoted mostly to Tracy and Suzi's efforts to get advances on their clothing allowance so they could buy new dresses for Saturday's Columbus Day dance.

I was going to the dance with Greg—at least I'd discovered that day that Greg was just assuming that we'd go together—but I wasn't concerned about what I would wear. I had too many other things on my mind.

The misty rain that had been pestering us on and off cleared during the night, and Thursday morning was all blue and gold with a hint of fall. The school bus passed through rolling countryside that made me homesick for Carlisle's Hope. If Aunt Faith were still alive, maybe we could have lived with her when—*if*—Dad and Mother went overseas.

"Let's eat outdoors," Alaiyo suggested to Stephanie and me when lunchtime came. Asagai was out on a national holiday, so Alaiyo didn't mind a girls-only lunch. We ate under the copper beech tree, just the three of us, and we didn't talk about any loaded subjects.

The afternoon warning bell rang, and we were still out there. Most of the other students had already moved indoors by the time we finished picking up our trash. We started around the side of the main building toward Evesham's front door, and I noticed a car under the trees with its motor running. It wasn't in the parking lot, but in the drive where bushes screened it from the school's front windows.

As we came up even with the car a man got out. He looked pleasant, middle-aged, and perfectly ordinary, but a prickle ran down my spine. Maybe it was because we weren't used to seeing strange men on the grounds. Maybe it was because of the car, idling and half hidden.

I linked my arm through Stephanie's and picked up speed. As I did so, the man stepped forward.

"Hello, Stephanie," he said.

Stephanie froze. I pushed her hard, veering toward the school. Alaiyo grabbed her other arm. "Come on, girl!" she said in a sharp undertone, and yanked her arm.

"It's all right," Stephanie said in a brittle voice. "It's my father." She didn't budge, but her hand slid down into mine and gripped it tightly. Alaiyo closed in, a protective guardian on Steff's other side. Steff didn't look at us. She was staring, absolutely expressionless, at her father.

I didn't even know his name. Stephanie supplied it. "Mr. Lawrence Holt. My two best friends." She did not identify us. Mr. Holt nodded toward us, but he didn't take his eyes off her.

"I didn't mean to frighten you," Mr. Holt said. "I thought—" He hesitated, then shrugged with the same slight shake of the head Stephanie often used. "I thought we needed to meet on our own, before tomorrow, so we could talk."

Behind us the bell for afternoon classes rang. I made a small involuntary movement. "Stay where you are, both of you," Stephanie ordered. "Anything he has to say to me he can say in front of you two."

Mr. Holt and I both spoke at once:

"Steff, don't you think—"

"We need to get to know—"

"*No,*" Stephanie said sharply. She seemed motionless, but as she looked at her father I could feel her trembling. "You've had plenty of time to try to get to know me," she said in that voice like cold silver. "Twelve years. In all the time since you and my mother split up, you never tried to see me. So why now? *No,*" she said harshly, as he tried to speak. "Whatever gave you the idea *I'd* want to see *you*? It's too late. I've had quite enough of fathers, thank you."

"Steff," I said gently, "don't you think—"

"He has no right to expect me to welcome him with open arms," Stephanie snapped. "He has no rights at all. Not after the way he's refused to have anything to do with bringing me up. And it's not just the child support he didn't pay. He hasn't sent me birthday or Christmas presents since I was ten."

Mr. Holt straightened and seemed to get taller. He said evenly, "That's not true."

He didn't say it angrily or with shock. He used that same cold, level voice that Stephanie was using, and it got to her. I knew it did.

She looked at him blankly and gave that little head shake, and Mr. Holt went on, never taking his eyes off hers. "The only time I missed any child-support payments was for three months right after the divorce, and that was because your mother had emptied my bank accounts before I could get them out of both our names. She wouldn't have told you about that because you were too young, but when she walked out, she took everything I had. I came home and found every stick of furniture gone from the apartment, all my family photographs and souvenirs, all the bankbooks and financial papers. It took me a year to get on an even keel again—in more ways than one."

"That isn't true," Stephanie said uncertainly. But she dropped her eyes.

"Isn't it?" her father asked quietly. "I wouldn't be saying these things to you, even now that you're grown, if it weren't that by now you surely must know Paulina."

"That was twelve years ago," Stephanie said,

childishly denying. "Whatever she did then—whatever she's ever done—*she's* had to raise me. She's had to support me. You didn't want to."

"That's not true either," Mr. Holt said gently. "Stephanie, I'm paying your tuition here. Ask the headmistress. I've paid child support regularly, through all Paulina's marriages, until she decided a year and a half ago that it was making Calvin Payne jealous. Look at her old bankbooks if you don't believe me. I sent you birthday presents and Christmas presents and holiday presents, too, in care of Paulina because she insisted."

And then she took the gift tags off before giving them to Stephanie, I thought sickly.

"When you were ten, I stopped picking the things out myself and just sent money, so your mother could do my shopping. She told me I didn't know how to choose things for a growing girl. I gather she never told you those presents came from me." Mr. Holt paused again. "I wrote you, but you never wrote back." Steff had never seen those letters, and I suspected he now realized it. "Your mother said it was because my letters upset you too much, and told me I should stop. I was traveling around the West Coast on business most of that time anyway, so having you visit would have been difficult for you. But I thought now that you were almost sixteen, it was time to try again. Was I wrong?"

Stephanie didn't answer, but two tears started

rolling slowly down her cheeks. She kept her head high, and we pretended not to see them.

"Incidentally," Mr. Holt added, "your mother has always known precisely where to reach me, including when she's had court orders out forbidding me from contacting you. I'm not trying to damage your mother in your eyes, Stephanie. She's not a bad woman. Only impulsive. And possessive."

A shudder ran through Stephanie again. Mr. Holt held out a handkerchief, smiling faintly. "Here. It won't compromise your loyalties to borrow this."

Stephanie took it, dried her eyes, and said to Alaiyo and me, very quietly, "Please tell the school office I'm missing classes this afternoon because I've gone for a ride with my father. There are things we have to talk about."

And she walked away from us to the car, and got in when her father opened the door for her.

"Well!" Alaiyo breathed profoundly as we watched the car move off. "You'd better give her mother a phone call. Only give Steff a break and don't do it till you get home from school."

"She isn't home anyway," I remembered, feeling relieved. "She rode into D.C. with my mother. Mom's on a writing assignment and Paulina's clothes shopping. They won't be home till six."

We started toward our classes, extremely late, and as we did so I suddenly heard a voice behind me, shouting.

"Jess!" It was Scott, and he was out of breath. He reached us in two bounds and grabbed my arms. "Have you seen John Henry? Nobody can find him. The principal called me to the office because they can't reach Mom or Dad, and John Henry's been missing since his second morning class!"

FOURTEEN

WITHIN MINUTES we were in the Cheltenham School office, Scott and I, and Alaiyo, who would not leave me, with the principal and vice-principal.

John Henry had attended his first two classes. He had not shown up afterward, and had been marked absent in class attendance books. It was not till one o'clock, when the vice-principal's secretary checked the morning class absences against the school's master attendance list for the day, that his disappearance had become known. A senior student on monitor duty had been sent to check all the places younger boys usually could be found when cutting classes. No John Henry.

"We've been trying to reach your parents, but your father's secretary says he's not available, and your mother isn't home."

"She's in D.C. on business. Have you checked the grounds? John Henry's used to living in the country, and he likes to go off alone when he's upset."

The vice-principal picked up an intercom phone. "I'll get some of the seniors out of class and organize a search."

"Get the Evesham seniors too," Alaiyo suggested. That phone call brought Tracy and Suzi flying over.

"Are any of the other boys missing?" the principal asked. "Usually when students cut, it's with their friends."

"John Henry doesn't have friends here yet. Except Greg. Maybe Greg knows where he may have gone."

So Greg, too, was summoned, but he shook his head. "That's part of the kid's problem. He feels like an outsider."

"We'll find him. He must still be on the grounds," the principal said kindly, seeing my expression. "There's no way he could have gotten far."

I thought of Stephanie and her father, just driving off, while Suzi gave the principal a disgusted look. "He could be hitchhiking. 'Borrowing' somebody's bike. Hiding in a delivery truck."

The principal frowned. "It's unfortunate no one's at your house, in case the boy shows up there."

I looked at Scott. "Caroline. Mother told her to keep the house key Bruce was using while he was baby-sitting Featherstone."

Greg grabbed the principal's phone without bothering to ask, and dialed his mother.

"I'll go right over," Caroline said immediately. "Bruce just walked in. I'll send him out to the school to drive you kids home."

While we were waiting the search of the school grounds got underway. Scott used the secretary's phone to try to track Dad down. I took the principal's and called *The Washington Post*. Mother had already been and gone. I called Clyde's. She wasn't there. I called Paulina. Paulina wasn't home. In between those calls I tried our own house and got Caroline. John Henry had not turned up.

Bruce arrived. We all, including Alaiyo, piled into his old car. Once outside the school gates Bruce broke speed limits, and it was a good thing we encountered no one on those hairpin turns.

Caroline had the coffeepot going by the time we arrived. "I wouldn't overreact if I were you," she said cheerfully. "John Henry strikes me as a very self-reliant young man." She turned to Greg.

"Where would you go if you were John Henry?"

Greg frowned. "Home. But John Henry clearly isn't here." We knew that; the first thing we'd done was check our house, with Featherstone's assistance, from attic to cellar.

"I don't think John Henry feels like this *is* home," Tracy said soberly. "I don't think he feels like any place is home, now that Aunt Faith's gone and Uncle Henry's back in Japan. I thought he was adjusting, but the past day or so he's been right back behind his walls."

"What's happened the past couple of days?" Caroline asked.

I looked at her, feeling sick. "Dad told us we're probably going to be shipped to the Middle East at a moment's notice."

Caroline looked shocked but recovered quickly. "Okay. He may think he has a responsibility to take himself off your hands. What would he do?"

"At his age," Greg said, "I'd have gone to somebody I didn't feel I'd be an imposition on."

"His father," Bruce said. We nodded. "But his old man's in Japan. That would take money. And a passport. He can't get those this fast."

Caroline frowned. "He must have a passport. Jenetta told me Faith and Henry and John Henry went to Italy last June. But he wouldn't have the passport here."

"You don't know John Henry. He's the kind

who always has his savings account passbook on him, so he can check it every couple of hours." I ran up to John Henry's room, and Scott followed.

There was a metal strongbox in John Henry's bureau drawer. Scott broke the lock without looking the least bit guilty. There was a touching assortment of treasures in it, but no passport.

"Which doesn't mean it *hadn't* been here," Scott said.

"He couldn't be trying to go to Japan. He doesn't have credit cards. He doesn't have the money." I wanted very much to believe that. "Even his savings account"—I picked up the passbook and flipped through it—"there isn't enough for Japan, and he can't get it out from here. He can't get it out, period, without this."

Scott looked at me. "Do you realize what else isn't here? His coin collection."

We rushed frantically downstairs. It was at this point that my parents walked in, within a few minutes of each other. Dad was with Ali, having received the message Scott had left with Ali's embassy. Mother was with Paulina. Tracy summed the situation up for them swiftly.

Dad grabbed the phone and handed Mom the phone book. "The Japan Air Lines number," he ordered Mother, "and then Pan Am. I know we don't know yet if he has the money, but we can't waste any time."

It was already four hours since John Henry had walked off.

"I'll check the coin store," Greg said, and vanished. He came back quickly. John Henry had not been in there to sell his coins, but the store owner had told Greg what John Henry could reasonably collect if he did sell them. The figure was greeted with a shocked and worried silence.

"Let me call Asagai," Alaiyo said abruptly. "He may have discussed coin dealers with John Henry." She was able to reach him. She spoke quickly. Another silence followed, punctuated by her exclamation.

"You did? He what? Yes. Yes, please do." She hung up. "Asagai bought the coins. John Henry called Tuesday night and asked him if he wanted to. He told Asagai his father would approve of it when he heard. So he must be trying to get to him. Asagai's coming over. And he's asked his father to get the embassy to put pressure on the airport and the airlines."

It dawned on Dad and Ali that they were in positions to apply pressure too. Ali took our phone first.

Caroline made more coffee. Featherstone went crazy trying to figure out who was in the most need of the comfort of his kisses. Asagai arrived. One of Scott's friends showed up from school to say the search of the grounds had been unsuccessful.

In the middle of all this Paulina looked at me. "Where's Stephanie?" she demanded. "Why didn't she come home with you to help?"

I looked right back at her and I said clearly, "She's gone off with her father to find out how many lies you've told her." And Paulina went into hysterics.

She went into hysterics in the middle of our frantic kitchen. She grabbed me and shook me and shouted about betrayal. Mother and Ali tried to pull her off, but I wrenched myself free and inside me something snapped.

"You call Stephanie's seeing her own father a betrayal? After all the other fathers you've shoved on her? After you've been telling her all these years how you've had to slave to support her, and how you'd never survive if you didn't keep on the hunt for rich husbands to look after you?"

"*Jessamyn!*" said Mother in a terrible voice. I ignored her.

"Mr. Holt—and it's a wonder Stephanie even knows his name—has been paying Stephanie's expenses all the time, hasn't he? He's been sending her presents, but you didn't tell her. God knows why! Were you afraid she might like him? Were you afraid she might want to get away from you? Didn't it ever occur to you Steff might find a father with flaws better than no father at all? Or maybe you just don't care whether she has any roots!"

Greg moved toward me and took my hand. I

burst into tears. Dad came in and tried to intervene.

"I won't stop," I said doggedly. "And I'm not sorry. Steff's right; being a minor can be awful. Especially when you don't have my kind of parents. Most people do things *to* kids or *for* kids, but the kids don't have any power. Not even to find their fathers when they vanish!"

I was talking not just about Stephanie, but about my grandfather and about John Henry. I turned on my father. "Uncle Henry's got to make it clear to John Henry that he hasn't dumped him. And you've got to make it clear that even if we get shipped out again, he still has a home."

"I thought he knew that," Dad said. "But you're right. People do need to be told." He gave me a pat on the shoulder.

"Oh, darling," Mother whispered to me.

Caroline thrust a glass of cold water into Paulina's hands. "Drink this. And sit down."

"I'm all right," Paulina said steadily. And indeed, she was surprisingly pulled together.

Maybe she has been afraid of losing Steff, I thought. Maybe now that the worst has happened, she'll have one thing less to fear. One thing I knew: Steff would not wash her hands of her mother; she had too much sense of responsibility. Like Great-grandmother Faith. Like Dad, bringing up Aunt Faith after his father died. Like me? I hoped so; I fervently did hope so. I had Faith Carlisle's blood in my veins, after all. And the Carlisle standards. *Up the Carlisles.*

Phone calls started coming in. Cheltenham, reporting no further news. The airlines, reporting no flight booked in his name.

Uncle Henry, from Japan, returning Dad's call.

Dad laid it on the line, being cruelly kind. "We're doing everything that can be done here. No, I'm sure he's not in any trouble. No, don't fly here! You have to stay in Tokyo in case he shows up there. But once we find him, Henry, you had better come, even if it has to be for only twenty-four hours. You and I have to talk, and you have to make it clear to your son that he *is* wanted, and exactly what plans you're making for him. And you'd better include him in the decision making!"

Up the Carlisles.

It would have done John Henry good to hear that. It would have done him good to see all the effort and caring that was being expended. Before he turned himself into a cold fish like Uncle Henry, he needed to know that his father, too, had feelings, and that hidden feelings only went underground; they didn't die.

Of course, what J. H. really needed—what Uncle Henry needed—was Aunt Faith. Aunt Faith, or her spirit, and the healing serenity of Carlisle's Hope.

I looked up slowly, and it was as if somewhere in my head I heard Aunt Faith speaking. And suddenly I knew exactly where John Henry was.

FIFTEEN

"John henry's gone to Carlisle's Hope," I heard my own voice say.

Everybody jumped. My father looked at me with surprised respect. "You're right. We should have thought of it. It's the logical place."

Mother was already on the telephone. "No answer," she said at last. "I let it ring and ring."

"Doesn't mean anything." Dad rose. "I can be there in three hours, driving. That's faster than fooling around with airports." He turned to me directly. "You want to come?"

"You know I do."

He didn't ask any of the others. And in spite of

the fact that Carlisle's Hope was a favorite of theirs, too, they didn't ask to go along.

"I'll fill the car up with gas," Tracy volunteered, and Mother tossed her the keys.

"Want me to call your office in the morning and cancel your appointments?" Scott asked Dad.

"Please. I'll phone you after we get out there and know what's what."

I still had my school uniform on. I ran upstairs to change into jeans and a sweater. I also phoned Gadge, which we should have done sooner. She hadn't heard a thing from John Henry. Mother got on the kitchen extension and persuaded Gadge to sit tight instead of flying here, in case John Henry showed up on her doorstep.

Dad called the airlines again, this time the ones that went to Florida.

"Bus tickets," Suzi said suddenly. "You know how tight that kid is with money. He might have taken off by bus and kept the rest of the cash to live on."

Greg started calling the bus lines, asking about a ten-year-old blond boy with glasses, wearing a Cheltenham uniform.

"Keep the phone lines clear," Dad ordered, reappearing, having changed into a plaid shirt and beat-up jeans of his own.

"If you can't reach us, phone Caroline," Mother told him. "We may have responses from all our search calls coming in."

Dad nodded.

The lights from the walleyed windows of the Flounder House glowed after us as we drove into the night.

The way to Carlisle's Hope was so familiar that we practically rode on automatic pilot. By now it was well past dark, and there were few cars on the Interstate. We didn't talk much; we didn't have to.

"How did you think of Carlisle's Hope?" Dad asked me eventually, and I told him the things I'd come to realize that "taking the name of Carlisle" meant. I didn't elaborate; I didn't have to.

Somewhere on the other side of the Baltimore tunnel our stomachs started reminding us that we'd had no dinner, so we stopped for hamburgers. We stopped again, for coffee, in a roadhouse on the outskirts of Philadelphia. Then we drove on.

We were off the Interstate now, and a worm of uneasiness began crawling through me. Suppose John Henry wasn't at Carlisle's Hope after all? Suppose he'd tried to hitchhike and had gotten in trouble? What could he do once he reached Carlisle's Hope? It was closed up, and he couldn't expect to live there on his own, could he? But then at John Henry's age logic wasn't always a factor.

We drove off the highway onto the familiar secondary road, and all the old landmarks sat quietly, shrouded by the dark. We turned down the narrow side road, and the Pennsylvania rail fences, the tall old trees, all spoke to me of memories. My eyes were stinging, and I closed them briefly. When I opened them we were turning into the drive to Carlisle's Hope.

The old house loomed up. There was a dim light coming through one of the lower windows, but that wasn't what made Dad say, in a tight kind of voice, "He's here."

The Carlisle clan banner was flying from the flagpole. We could see it by the faint moonlight, vaguely stirring in an errant breeze.

"We don't want to startle him," Dad said, so we parked the car, got out quietly, and tried the front door. It was bolted. I know that because Dad tried the credit-card-in-the-door jamb stunt, after swearing at himself for not having gotten a set of house keys from Uncle Henry, and the card trick didn't work.

"There has to be a way in," I pointed out. "John Henry got in."

Dad and I looked at each other, then split up to circle the house and look for unlocked doors or open windows. Nothing was open except the window of John Henry's bedroom. Dad eyed it, and I shook my head.

"The only way to reach it is up the ivy vine, and it won't hold either of us." I did not explain how I knew this, and Dad didn't ask, but I saw a smile tug at the corner of his mouth.

"John Henry doesn't need to wake up to a monster face in his window anyway," he said. "He was reading my *Complete Sherlock Holmes* and *Complete Works of Edgar Allan Poe* last week."

I saw his point. But there had to be a way in, because J. H. had found it. I looked at my father, and found him looking at me with a speculative half smile.

"Jess," he said slowly, "are you by any chance familiar with the coal cellar?"

I grinned back. "Scott showed it to us years ago. The cellars here are a great place to play Dungeons and Dragons in." I should have remembered that sooner, because John Henry had played with us.

The cellars of Carlisle's Hope were a warren of connecting spaces, added on as the house had been enlarged for each succeeding generation. The floors were hard-packed earth, the walls were stone. Sometime in the mid-nineteenth century the newfangled central heating had been introduced, and with its coming the original single cellar had been transformed into a coal storage bin. It had one of those sloping wood trapdoors outside the house, with a flight of stairs to the cellar. And, more important, a square hole, waist-high, that opened into the main cellar room, where the furnace stood. That hole was intended for coal, but it could accommodate a child. Or a very small adult.

I didn't spare a thought for my sweater. I was

already trying the trapdoor. The wood was rotting, and the padlock had been forced.

I stumbled down the stairs, cursing because we hadn't brought a flashlight. Then I groped my way to the nearest wall and, by following it with my hands, found the small opening.

Now what? Going through it headfirst did not appeal to me, and I didn't know how to get through any other way.

"I'm here, Jess," Dad said behind me. He had followed me down.

He hoisted me up, and between us we maneuvered me feetfirst through the crawl hole. It was a *very* tight fit. Dad eased me down. My feet touched the hard-packed floor.

"There's a light switch at the top of the stairs," Dad said. "Feel your way. There's a lot of junk down here."

I didn't need reminding. I groped along again, through the furnace room, through the room beyond where old furniture was kept. I found the stairs. I counted the seventeen steps. I flipped on the light.

The cellar, with its centuries of Carlisle history, sprang into view. I tried the door at the top of the stairs, and it was locked. I could have cried.

"There are screwdrivers in the toolbox," Dad called. "Jimmy the doorframe. That's only an old, flimsy lock, and it will give."

I was uncovering all kinds of skills I hadn't

known I had. But after all, the Carlisles were survivors, weren't we? I grinned to myself as I went round to let Dad in through the back door. The kitchen showed signs that a makeshift meal had been prepared.

"Look," Dad said, and pointed to the dining room. Somebody had dined there alone, and I do mean dined. There was one of Aunt Faith's crystal goblets, and one of her old Spode plates, and it looked as though candles had been lit.

We tiptoed upstairs, avoiding creaks, and there was John Henry, tucked into his own bed. Dad woke him gently.

"If you were planning an excursion, old man, you might have invited me along," he said mildly as John Henry did a double-take and rubbed his eyes.

"I didn't want you to have to feel responsible for me," John Henry said. "You have enough to be responsible for already. Going overseas again and all."

I swallowed hard. Dad didn't bat an eye. "You can't help my feeling responsible for you," he said. "Not because of overseas duty. And not because you're underage and your own dad's in Japan. I feel responsible for you because I care about you. Didn't you feel responsible for your mother, even though you were a kid and she was the parent? Aren't you *still* feeling responsible for what happened to her?"

Whammo. Right between the eyes. I heard

John Henry gulp, and I heard my father say, "It's okay. I went through it too." And I got out of there fast, because I *hadn't* gone through it—losing a parent, I mean.

I went downstairs, and *I* lit candles. I put the kettle on. I went to the freezer and took out one of the special raspberry cakes Aunt Faith had made last summer.

And I cried.

I had gotten myself in hand though, by the time Dad and John Henry, also now dry-eyed, came downstairs. It occurred to us then to phone Mother, and tell her to call off the Marines, the world was safe.

"We'll be back tomorrow afternoon," Dad said. "John Henry wants time to pack some of his things to bring along. He's decided he'll stay with us at least till the end of this school semester. After that we'll see what's developed. He might like the experience of living overseas if the opportunity arises."

Dad and John Henry lit a fire in the big old kitchen fireplace, and we sat by it drinking herbal tea and eating cake. We talked about Aunt Faith, and about the few years Dad had lived here after she was born. "I wasn't much older than you, come to think of it," Dad said.

"Weren't you scared?" John Henry asked. "When you had to become the man of the family, I mean?"

"Sure, I was scared. But being brave doesn't mean not being scared, it means going on anyway."

"Like the Carlisle motto," John Henry agreed.

"What made you come here?" I put in, and John Henry looked at me as though I were stupid.

"It's the family homestead, isn't it? Mom said that's what homestead means—a place that all the kin can come to whenever they need. I knew I could get in. I figured I could live on the coin money for a while, and then do odd jobs for people around here till my dad got back."

"I'm surprised you didn't think of investing the money in the stock market and living off your profits," Dad said respectfully, and John Henry looked interested. "Just as a matter of curiosity, didn't you think it might be thoughtful to let us know what you were up to, so we wouldn't worry?"

"I mailed you a letter," John Henry said. "This morning, from the bus station. I didn't," he pointed out logically, "want you to find out before I got here or you'd think you couldn't let me come."

Exactly what I would have done—and Dad, too, I suspected.

"And dinner in the dining room?" I asked gently.

John Henry looked surprised. "We always eat dinner in the dining room."

Of course, I thought. The Carlisles lit candles.

The Carlisles flew their banner. The Carlisles, come what may, survived. It wasn't a matter of bloodline, or of tradition only. It was a matter of patterning, passed on in love; a way of not only surviving but of triumphing, and with not only guts but with grace.

That was what being a Carlisle—being a family—really meant. Having a taproot that could not be severed. It wasn't dependent on proximity or geography any more than it was dependent on genetics. And if it was something that transcended generations, then even death, as the saying goes, could not be proud.

For the first time I could glance toward Aunt Faith's self-portrait in the hall without hurting.

We went to bed at last, and when I awakened in the familiar room, the sun was shining. There was a smell of coffee perking. And, astonishingly, there was the sound of somebody hammering the knocker of the front door.

I ran to the window and leaned out. And then I gasped.

"Wait a minute! I'll be right down!"

I careened down the stairs, colliding with my father in the front hall. "I'll get it!" I gasped, and spun the heavy bolt and flung the old door open. And there was Greg Barillo, sauntering in as if he'd been doing so all his life.

"What are you doing here?" my father demanded with a smile.

"I caught the red-eye bus to Philadelphia and then hitchhiked. Thought I could help John Henry get his gear together and maybe he or somebody would show me around the farm. I hear it's really something."

"'Or somebody,'" John Henry echoed, appearing on the staircase, grinning.

"Okay, okay, I'll give you the guided tour," I said. "After breakfast. Maybe we'll have time for a horseback ride. We have to get back for that dance tonight, remember?"

I could have sworn I heard Aunt Faith chuckling as I swept toward the kitchen, my kin—of blood and spirit—around me. Behind us in the front yard the Carlisle banner lifted in the early sun.

Up the Carlisles!

AUTHOR'S NOTE

JESSAMYN CARLISLE, her immediate family and her friends, are all fictional characters. However her grandfather, William Charles Edwards Carlisle, is based on my own father, Charles Eugene Chambers Johnston. Faith Dryden Edwards Carlisle is my grandmother, Catherine A. I. Dryden Chambers Johnston, and Jess's Great-grandmother Faith's story is Catherine's story. William Edwards is my grandfather, Charles W. Chambers, and Douglas Scott Carlisle is a totally fictional version of my step-grandfather, Edward Johnston (Johnson).

All three of these died before I was born. If

any readers can supply me with any information on the Edmundsons, Drydens, Chamberses, and Johnstons (Johnsons) who lived in Pittsburgh, Pennsylvania, between 1895 and 1942 (or later), I would be very happy to receive it. And of course, I'd be glad to hear from other readers as well!

Norma Johnston
Dryden Harris St. John, Inc.
% AMS
103 Godwin Ave.
Midland Park, New Jersey 07432-0060

ABOUT THE AUTHOR

NORMA JOHNSTON is the author of over sixty books for adults and young adults, including the acclaimed Keeping Days series. Ms. Johnston has many different interests, from theater, gourmet cooking, and history to psychology, folksongs, and computers. She has traveled extensively around the world, from Europe to the Middle East.

Ms. Johnston's varied career has included being a teacher, actress and play director, boutique owner, and freelance editor. About her highly successful writing career, she says: "Why do I write? Because I have things that I must say—in person, over a pot of tea before the fire, on stage, in print—and I can no more hold back from saying them than I can cease to breathe."

She is currently at work on two gothic mysteries for the Bantam Starfire line.

A special preview of the exciting
opening chapter of the second book
in the fabulous new trilogy:

THE CARLISLE CHRONICLES

Book 2

TO JESS, WITH LOVE
AND MEMORIES

by Norma Johnston

It all started with one of our "family discussions." That's what they're usually referred to as around our house—either tongue in cheek or with a hollow laugh. The label started three years ago when my older sister, Tracy, now a high school senior, played the title role in the Cheltenham-Evesham schools' production of *The Diary of Anne Frank*. There's a place in the play where Anne is dumbfounded at the decibel range of the Van Daan family fights, and Mr. Van Daan bellows, "This isn't an argument, it's a *discussion!*" That's the kind of family discussions we Carlisles are prone to having. Not surprising, maybe, when you figure that besides me, Jessamyn Faith (Jess for short; I'm fifteen), there's Tracy Louise (seventeen), Scott Thomas (sixteen, and an electronics genius), and Susan Clare (Suzi, who's thirteen). Plus my parents, who are not exactly inhibited or introverted, and my ten-year-old cousin, John Henry Squier, who's an add-on. John Henry *is* introverted—and inhibited, ever since his mother, my beloved aunt

Faith, died in an auto accident a month ago. But in the month since he arrived (John Henry's father is stationed overseas), he's rapidly been learning to hold his own.

Our family discussions can erupt without warning, last for days (despite Mother's family motto about never letting the sun go down on your anger), and range up and down the four floors—not to mention attic and cellar—of our house in Old Town, Alexandria, Virginia. They scare the wits out of my friend Stephanie Payne, who's the only child of a much-divorced mother (*their* fights are laden with silences, crying jags, and hysterics). Most of the time these discussions roll right off the backs of us Carlisles, having cleared the air and given everyone a refreshing dose of adrenaline.

Sometimes the discussions are catastrophic.

The one on Friday, the twenty-fifth of October, was catastrophic. It shook my world, and the horrible part was that neither Suzi nor I meant for that to happen. What was frightening was that it was so totally without warning—like the summer we were all out at Carlisle's Hope in Pennsylvania when we were small, and my brother, Scott, found a funny stone and flung it in the cookout fire. Only it hadn't been a stone but some kind of explosive left over from the Fourth of July. It had gone off at close range and scarred Scott's face forever.

Oh, not so badly that he did not still look like Scott; in fact, you had to get close and stare hard to see the marks, because the doctor did a good patch-up job. But they're there, they'll always be there, and Scott can't forget. That's the way it is for me now.

On second thought, if Suzi and I had not been so pigheaded, we might have known if not where, at least to what kind of trouble, our clash would lead. I was trying to pull rank while our parents were away. Suzi was trying to prove she could not be dominated, least of all by me.

Unfortunately our family traits got in the way of reason. Those traits come from both sides of the family—from Dad's Carlisles and Drydens and Edmundsons and Sterlings; from Mother's Pilgrim Standishes and Jersey Dutch Vandevers and Italian Rienzis. Both sides of our heritage collided with the impact of a bomb that afternoon.

I'm getting ahead of myself. Suzi and I were holding the fort in the Flounder House, our funny old home in Alexandria, because my father, Douglas Edward Carlisle, who's a Senior Service Officer with the U.S. Information Agency, had to fly to Paris again for a long weekend, and he persuaded my mother to go with him. "For crying out loud, Jenetta, Tracy will be away in college next year, and Scott's been dependable since he was in kindergarten. Certainly they should be old enough to keep an eye on Jess and Suzi and John Henry for three days. If we can't trust them all by now, when are we ever going to be able to?"

"Suzi," my mother had said with meaning.

"That's what I meant by when are we ever going to be able to?" Dad said ruefully.

"We could stay at the Barillos'," Tracy said innocently. "I'm sure Caroline would take us in."

"With a little help from her friends?" Mother asked with a gleam in her eye. She was referring to Tracy's passionate romance with Caroline's college-student son, Bruce. Not to mention my own involvement with Bruce's younger brother, Greg. Mother had no idea (I hope) whether that was passionate or not (it wasn't yet, but not for lack of interest on either part). Being no fool, she wasn't taking any chances. "I'd sooner let you guys stay here by yourselves," she said.

"So then let them," Dad said reasonably. "Think about having a late dinner, just the two of us, in that little café on the Left Bank."

"Late would not be unusual. Alone with you would," Mother retorted. But a smile began to twitch at the corners of her mouth.

That had been at dinner Wednesday evening.

On Thursday night our parents boarded the plane for Paris at National Airport. It was on Friday that the buildup to explosion began.

The first thing that happened was that I was flagged down in the corridor at school by Mrs. Tarrant, who is the math teacher for the junior high at the private school we Carlisles attend, and an old buddy of mine. "Jess, can I talk to you a minute?" she asked. "What's going on with Suzi?"

"What do you mean?" Out of habit I stalled for time. Such openings, where Suzi was concerned, were ominous. Mrs. Tarrant laughed, but her eyes were serious.

"Don't worry, she hasn't been caught smoking pot, and she hasn't cut a class yet this year. She also hasn't been doing any work. The marking period's closing next week, and she has two F's. And one D-minus, which was stretching some, because she answered only ten out of twenty problems. If I'm going to go out on a limb for her, I have to know she's at least going to make an effort."

"Math's never been easy for her."

"I know that. And I know about the learning disability that didn't get diagnosed when it should have because you had to keep changing schools in the Middle East. I also know that Suzi has twice had appointments to work with me after school, and has not shown up, and that she hasn't handed in half of her assignments. I hate to report it to the principal," Mrs. Tarrant said frankly, "because after the troubles she was in over missed work last year, she's only back this year on probation." That was something I *hadn't* known. "If she doesn't pass a make-up test—and hand in her back homework—by next Friday, she'll fail for the marking period and be out on her ear."

"Thanks. I'll talk to her," I murmured, my stomach knotting. Suzi did not take kindly to sisterly lectures, but she'd take even less kindly to the way an F on her report card would strike my parents. Last June, when her final grades had been two D-minuses, one C, and the rest D's, Dad had sworn to pack her off to an uptight, noncoed boarding school if it occurred again. Suzi had threatened suicide and running away, in that order, and we had had quite a family discussion.

It would be a very good idea for Suzi and me to have a private one now, just the two of us, while our parents were away.

I did not enjoy the rest of that day in school.

It was a weird day anyway. For one thing the boys weren't there. Cheltenham and Evesham are, respectively, all-male and all-female schools, but they share the same grounds, sometimes the same classes, and a lot of other things besides. This fall a crowd consisting of us Carlisles and all our friends has begun to eat lunch in whichever cafeteria has the more interesting food. That day the upper-class boys (including Scott, Greg Barillo, and Asagai, who's my friend Alaiyo's boyfriend) were away on a field trip. Tracy was eating with a couple of other senior girls. Suzi avoided me, which meant she could have gotten wind of my discussion with Mrs. Tarrant. And Stephanie was still away.

Stephanie is the subject of a belated and bitter custody fight between her mother, Paulina, and Paulina's second husband. Steff scarcely knows her own father, and has recently discovered that most of what she did know was a pack of lies told to her by Paulina. She went for a long-weekend reunion visit with him over Columbus Day, and had not yet returned, so Alaiyo and I had lunch alone together.

The talk went from Asagai to Steff and her family problems to Steff's mother's problems to my sister Suzi.

"Did you know she was over at the Jazz Club last night at ten P.M.?" Alaiyo asked.

"I did not. And you can bet ten dollars my parents didn't either. They were already on the plane to Paris. Scott drove them to the airport, and

I don't know when he got back, because I was in bed. I thought Suzi was in bed too."

"She wasn't." Alaiyo hesitated. "Look, I don't want to upset you, but some of the kids she was with were pretty gross."

"They would be," I said grimly. "How did she get in the place anyway?" The Jazz Club is a wine bar in Old Town that has great music and is off limits to high school students. I frowned. "Come to think of it, how did you get in? Not to mention how did you get *out* of the house on a school night?"

Alaiyo tossed her cornrows and tried to look like a Senegalese princess. "Asagai's a diplomat's son. And he looks twenty-one. Actually he *is* older than the rest of the seniors." I nodded. The main reason so many of us Foreign Service brats are in private schools is because the mixture of school curriculums we've gone through has left us out of sync with traditional grades and age levels. "Anyway" —Alaiyo reverted to what she was, the descendant of a long line of distinguished black American lawyers and Presbyterian ministers—"my parents don't know either. Asagai's parents asked me to dinner because his older sister's here for a few days. We stopped at the Jazz Club on the way home to have cappuccino and listen to a set. And we saw Suzi."

"Tell me the worst," I said grimly.

"Don't worry," Alaiyo said as Mrs. Tarrant had. "She was drinking Diet Coke and she wasn't smoking anything. But the guys at her table had been." She let the sentence hang significantly as I groaned.

The bell signaling the end of lunch period rang, to my relief. So I went to afternoon classes—at least my body did. My mind was not there. I was envisioning, all too clearly, the discussion I was going to have with Suzi. Because I was going to have to have it, wasn't I? *I* knew these things. *I* was her older sister. I didn't want to tattle, but that meant either *I* had to find a way to get through to my crazy sister or *I* would bear the responsibility for the consequences on my shoulders.

I didn't want Suzi to go through either of the consequences—being found out or getting burned. And I could not shrug it off as not my problem. All my instincts, all my heredity, rose up to protest that that was not the Carlisle way.

* * *

Would you like to read more? TO JESS, WITH LOVE AND MEMORIES will be available in July 1986. It will be on sale wherever Bantam paperbacks are sold. Outside the United States and Canada, books will be available approximately three months later. Check with your local bookseller for further details.

STARFIRE

More good STARFIRE books for teenagers —from Bantam Books

☐ **GENTLEHANDS**   23004/$2.25
  by M. E. Kerr
  *When a dark secret in his family's past is suddenly re-
  vealed, Buddy finds out that his Grandfather is the notori-
  ous Nazi war criminal, Gentlehands. By the author of
  Dinky Hocker Shoots Smack and Little, Little.*

☐ **WITH A FACE LIKE MINE,**   13921/$2.25
  YOU SETTLE FOR PERSONALITY
  by Sharon L. Berman
  *Thirteen-year-old Raina-Ann is absolutely filled with
  envy when she meets beautiful and sophisticated Arielle.
  But as their friendship grows, so to does Raina-Ann's
  self-image.*

☐ **WINNING**   25031/$2.50
  by Robin Brancato
  *When a disastrous football injury puts Garry Madden in a
  wheelchair forever, it takes everything he's got, plus a
  little help from a friend, to handle the changes in his life
  and come up a winner.*

☐ **HARRY AND HORTENSE**   25175/$2.95
  AT HORMONE HIGH
  by Paul Zindel
  *Harry and Hortense, students at chaotic Hormone High,
  don't know if Jason "Icarus" Rohr is the hero they've
  been waiting for—or a total madman. But from the very
  first it's clear that knowing Jason will change their lives
  forever. By the author of The Pigman and My Darling, My
  Hamburger.*

☐ **ALL TOGETHER NOW**   24530/$2.25
   by Sue Ellen Bridges

Casey had never lied before, at least not a big lie. But to save her friendship with Dwayne, she was ready to do anything. Even if it meant keeping a secret that would last the whole summer long. By the author of Home Before Dark *and* Notes For Another Life.

Stories of Love That Will Live Forever

☐ **JANE EYRE**   21140/$1.95
by Charlotte Bronte
JANE EYRE is about a young girl's awakening to life and to love. We see her grow from a shy schoolgirl to a spirited young governess who does not let class barriers keep her from falling in love with her employer, the arrogant, brooding Mr. Rochester. This is a book to treasure.

☐ **WUTHERING HEIGHTS**   21141/$1.95
by Emily Bronte
This is the timeless story of Cathy, a beautiful heiress and Heathcliff, a stormy, driven orphan who share one of the great loves of all time—and the ghost of this love will haunt Wuthering Heights forever.

☐ **LITTLE WOMEN**   21115/$2.95
by Louisa May Alcott
Quite simply, no young girl should grow up without reading this story of four very different girls. Meg, Jo, Beth and Amy struggle against their poverty with irresistible charm and good nature. The twists and turns their lives take will have you laughing and crying throughout.

DON'T MISS THESE OTHER SCARY BANTAM THRILLERS!